The Armageddon Twins

Jan-Andrew Henderson

Black Hart
Edinburgh. Brisbane.

Published by Black Hart, Edinburgh 2022
First published Floris Books, Edinburgh 2018
(As *It's Only the End of the World*).
ISBN: 9780192719577

Black Hart Entertainment.
www.blackhartentertainment.com

Cover by Panagiotis Lampridis (BookDesignStars)
Book Layout © 2017 BookDesignTemplates.com

The Armageddon Twins.
ISBN: 978-0-6452722-7-7
ISBN: 978-0-6452722-8-4 eBook

Praise for *The Armageddon Twins*

A whirlwind of action and breathless exposition…
A sharply built adventure with engaging characters.
Kirkus Reviews

Five parts of thrilling storytelling that is page turn-
ingly brilliant! Full of drama, unexpected twists,
genuine heartfelt moments and ACTUAL LOLS! Perfectly paced and wonderfully written. Daffodil
McNugget is inspired - Her one-liners are epic! If anyone needed another reason why J A Henderson is my
favourite author, then just read this book.
*Sharon Rooney (My Mad Fat Diary. The Electri-
cal Life of Louis Wain. Barbie)*

This book is a Hollywood holiday blockbuster, giant box of popcorn with your mates, having a good
time romp… And the clown sequence is inspired.
Armadillo Book Review Magazine

Chapters

The development of full artificial intelligence could spell the end of the human race... It would take off on its own and re-design itself at an ever-increasing rate. Humans, who are limited by slow biological evolution, couldn't compete, and would be superseded.

Stephen Hawking

One of the symptoms of an approaching nervous breakdown is the belief that one's work is terribly important.

Bertrand Russell. *The Conquest of Happiness*

For Caleb

One Month Earlier

Gerry Ray crouched in one corner, barely hidden behind a chrome console, sweating face pressed against the cold metal. An unconscious girl lay on the floor beside him.

A group of men and women in white coats were making their way through the room, oblivious to his presence. In the centre of the crowd marched a stout, middle-aged woman - the others were practically falling over each other to please her. Small wonder. She was the Vice President of Manticorps and her foul temper was legendary.

"We've recently made huge advances in the Marginal Science Projects, Miss Magdalene," a tall man said excitedly. "It's the reason we…"

"*Mrs* Magdalene," the woman interrupted.

"Oh. I didn't think anyone would marr…"

"We felt it best for you to witness the results in person." The lead scientist elbowed him out of the way. "It's all top secret and what we've achieved is nothing short of extraordinary."

"Make it quick, then." Mrs Magdalene looked at her watch. "I've got tickets for *Miss Saigon* and it starts in an hour."

She pressed her pass key to the lock, the door slid open with a hiss and the human convoy vanished into a corridor.

Gerry Ray waited until they were well out of ear-shot. Then he got on the nearest computer and began to type.

Why are you still inside the building, Gerry? A metallic voice crackled out of the computer speaker. *You should have found what you came for and made your escape by now.*

"There's been a hiccup, Nostradamus. The research team came back unexpectedly and almost caught me." The man scowled. "Thought you might have noticed something like that."

I took myself offline while you corrupted Manti-corps databases. Y'know. Just in case you wiped me by mistake.

"I'm not an idiot." Gerry finished typing with a flourish. "See? I've overloaded the systems in the east wing."

You did what?

"It fused the doors. Mrs Magdalene and her crew are trapped in their own labs."

Then get out of there now. The voice said urgently. *I'll take it from here.*

"Wasn't intending to hang around." Gerry hoisted the girl into his arms, staggered down the corridors and out of the building.

As he stumbled across the car park, there was a dull whump behind him. He skidded to a halt and turned.

A plume of fire was billowing from the roof of the Marginal Science Division and he could hear muffled screaming from the flaming interior.

"Oh, my God."

Gerry Ray bundled the girl into the boot of his stolen car.

"Nostradamus? What the hell have you done?"

-Part 1-

The Shake Up

A lot of people try to shape the future. Parents. Governments. Bankers. The police.

But it's the young ones who live in it. And we will fight for it.

Matt Wolfe.

-1-

Charlie Ray huddled under the covers, listening to the stranger hiding in his cupboard. He'd woken when he heard the window slowly slide up. The creak of a floorboard and the click of the door softly closing convinced him he wasn't dreaming. Now a strange crunching noise emanated from the closet.

He opened one eye and saw the digital clock read 3.00 am. Far too late for any of his friends to be playing a stupid prank. Anyway, he didn't have any friends.

Charlie lay perfectly still, pretending to be asleep, forcing his breathing to remain rhythmic. A month ago, he would have pulled the pillow over his head and curled into a ball, hoping the intruder would leave him alone.

Not anymore. The only thing that scared Charlie these days was himself.

His mother was sleeping in the next room but he had no intention of shouting for help. She wasn't exactly the 7th Cavalry and there was no way he was going to put her in any kind of danger.

This was his problem and he would deal with it.

He remained motionless, calculating what would be most useful as a weapon. There was a guitar on its stand by the window. A baseball bat leaning against the bookcase and a baseball blue-tacked to the second shelf. A heavy paperweight on his computer desk.

Charlie threw back the covers and rolled across the floor. He grabbed the bat and sprang to his feet, clutching it in both hands.

Pthhhhhp.

He blinked rapidly.

"You in there." He looked incredulously at the closed door. "Did you just... *fart?*"

"Couldn't help it," a muffled voice retorted. "I'm scrunched up like an accordion."

From the light of the moon, Charlie could see the key was still sticking out of the cupboard lock. He marched over and swiftly turned it. The handle rattled a few times, then stopped.

"Oops."

"Yeah. You're trapped, whoever you are," Charlie announced. "Now I'm going to call the police."

"Good luck with that, buster," the voice scoffed. "Your smartphone is in here with me. I'm lookin at your photo gallery right now."

Charlie glanced at the desk where he had left his mobile. It was gone.

"*Why?*"

"Cause it's boring in the closet and I wanted to have some light entertainment while I ate my crisps. What's a Prawn Cocktail, anyhow?"

Charlie heard the sound of a cellophane packet being scrunched.

"I'm finished now," the voice continued. "So open this door or I'm gonna post that baby video online that your mom took of you peeing on her couch."

"Why are you doing this to me?" Charlie's head was spinning. "Who *are* you?"

"Just let me out. I ain't gonna harm anyone."

"I'm going to fetch my mum and she can call the cops on *her* phone."

"You might find it a smidge difficult to rouse her," the voice apologised. "I was told to put a few sleeping pills in her cocoa, so she wouldn't disturb us."

"You did *what*?" Charlie's jaw tightened. "Nobody messes with my mum. Not after all she's been through. Nobody!"

He unlocked the door and yanked it open, bat raised above his head.

A girl burst out of the darkness and crashed into him. Charlie landed on his back with a grunt, the intruder squarely on top.

"Surprise!"

The girl giggled, then got quickly to her feet. Charlie stared in amazement as she did an awkward little dance on the spot.

"Gotta go to the ladies' room," she gasped. "Had a whole bottle of coke before I got here. 1.5-litre size."

"It's… at the end of the landing." Charlie was too taken aback to say anything else.

"Back in two shakes." She hobbled out of the door. "Nice tartan jim-jams, by the way."

When she returned, Charlie had pulled on a dressing gown and was sitting cross-legged on the bed, tapping the baseball bat into his palm.

He studied the stranger carefully. She was a well-built girl with cold blue eyes and a round face, framed by a glossy, shoulder-length bob. She wore a red top, short skirt and large black boots over crimson striped tights. He supposed she was quite pretty, in an odd sort of way, and looked about the same age as him.

"That's better." She wiped crumbs from her face and grinned, revealing a huge gap between her front teeth. "I should have gone before I climbed up your drainpipe. Must have a bladder the size of a pea."

Her accent was decidedly odd, not quite placeable, as if she were reading words from a script. The phraseology, however, reminded him of old western movies his father, Gerry, used to make him watch.

But he didn't like to think about his dad. Not if he could help it.

"Why were you in my cupboard?" he demanded.

"Nobody but you can know I'm here, see? I had to hide until I was sure your mom was out cold." The stranger shrugged. "Sides, I thought it would be funny."

"Do I look like I'm laughing?"

"You sure don't seem the jolly type," the girl muttered. "I reckon your face would slide off if you tried to raise a smile."

"*Excuse* me?"

"The name's Daffodil McNugget." She held out her hand. When Charlie refused to shake, she stuck a finger up his nose.

"Quit that!" He batted her away. "I want some answers or I *will* call the police."

"All right, grumpy." Daffodil backed off. "A voice in my head told me how to find you, so I could pass on an important message. Happy now?"

"That explains a lot." Charlie clutched the home-made weapon tighter. "You must have escaped from a funny farm."

"Ooooh. I like the sound of that!" Daffodil nodded approvingly. "Do the animals wear paper hats? Wait. Are they made of balloons?"

"Oh, dear God."

"Relax, will you?" She rolled her eyes. "I'm only joshin."

"Stop joshin and start explaining, before I wallop you with this bat. Who the hell *are* you?"

"That's a real thorny subject. See, I don't actually *remember* who I am." Daffodil scratched her temple uncertainly. "In fact, I don't remember much at all."

"Is that why you made up such a daft name?"

"You're one smart cookie, Chaz!" she beamed. "Howd'ya figure it out?"

Charlie jerked his thumb at a bunch of yellow flowers his mum had plonked on the dresser to brighten the room. Next to it was an empty carton of Chicken McNuggets.

"Ah." Daffodil pulled a face. "That obvious, huh?" She looked at him quizzically.

"Ain't you even a little curious why I'm here?"

"I'd be a lot more curious if it wasn't the middle of the night." Charlie rubbed his eyes. Now that he could see the girl wasn't some mugger, he was more annoyed than alarmed.

"Right now, I'm leaning towards escorting you out the front door, using the toe of my boot. My neighbour has a four-year-old. Go hide in his wardrobe, if you're into that kind of thing."

"Wise guy, huh?" Daffodil adjusted her tights, then smoothed down her skirt while Charlie tried not to stare. "I already said I'm here cause I got a message for you."

"From an imaginary voice in your head."

"Nothing imaginary about him," she corrected. "He's called Nostradamus and he knows *everything*."

Her voice lowered in admiration.

"He told me what an accordion was and how to post pictures online. I should ask him about crisp flavours next."

"The four-year-old next door could tell you all that." Charlie pointed his bat at her. "Get out of my house. I won't tell you again."

"Whatever." Daffodil gave a disdainful sniff and turned to go. "But the message ain't from Nostradamus. It's from a guy called Gerry Ray."

Charlie was off the bed in an instant.

"Wait!" He grabbed her arm. "*What* did you say?"

"The message is from a guy called Gerry Ray," she repeated. "Hey. You've both got the same last name! Is he some kind of relative?"

"Gerry Ray is my father." Charlie steered Daffodil to his computer chair and sat her down. When he let go, his hands were shaking.

"I haven't seen him since he walked out on us."

-2-

"I don't recall my own mom or pop," Daffodil said sadly. "So I been makin up stories in my head about them. There's not a lot to do in a closet."

She gave a heartfelt sigh.

"I don't even know if they're alive or…."

"My dad up and left last month," Charlie interrupted. "Cleared out our bank accounts. Didn't say goodbye or even leave me a note."

"Oh, I *do* apologise." Daffodil looked down at her outfit. "I don't know what day of the week it is and had to make up a name for myself a minute ago. What am *I* complaining about?"

"Just give me the message." Charlie held out his hand.

"Whatever you say. But I need a computer."

"Eh?" He pointed. "There's one next to your elbow."

"Of course. That's what the odd lookin box is." Daffodil rested her hand on top of the PC and its screen lit up. "I'm still getting used to new stuff."

"You didn't even switch it on." Charlie stared at her. "How is that possible?"

"Ain't got a clue. I didn't even know what a mobile was till Nostradamus told me. He's the only way I find out anything." She scratched her head. "Had to do a runner from the taxi that brought me here cause I didn't know I was supposed to pay."

But Charlie wasn't listening, for a familiar face appeared on the monitor.

Gerry Ray was sitting attentively, hands clasped on his lap, as if he had been waiting there for some time. He looked nervous and exhausted. His normally neat hair was dyed platinum and he had a bushy moustache to match. His usual shirt and tie had been replaced by a yellow tee-shirt and jeans and he wore a bandana around his neck.

"Dad!" Charlie gasped. "It's really you! Where have you been?"

I got so much to say, my boy. The man smiled wanly. *And so little time to say it. But let's start with how much I love you.*

"You got a funny way of showing it," Charlie shot back. "Mum's been in bits since you left. Me too, for that matter."

I had no choice, son. I'm in hiding. It's the reason for this disguise.

"That's a disguise?" Daffodil sniffed. "I thought a seagull crashed into his face."

"Hiding from what?" Charlie pushed the girl away. "Unpaid parking tickets? You work as a web designer and live in suburbia."

He glanced at the room next to his.

"I should wake mum."

No! His father held up a hand. *I have a story to tell you and I need to make it quick. Nostradamus is jamming this signal but every second I talk increases the chances that the people bugging your house will grow suspicious.*

"Our house isn't bugged!" Charlie couldn't hide his disbelief. "That's crazy talk."

Son. Gerry Ray cut him short. *Please listen. All our lives depend on it.*

That shut Charlie up.

A while ago, I stole something extremely valuable from some very nasty people and they'll do anything to get it back. That's why I had to go on the run.

"So return whatever it was," Charlie snapped. "I've been worried sick."

I would if I could, but it's not an option. However, if they knew I'd been in touch, or even cared what happened to you and mum, they'd whisk you both away. Hold you hostage to flush me out of hiding.

He looked mortified.

I had to make it seem like I'd completely abandoned you, for your own safety.

His voice lowered

Please. Let me tell you what happened. No interruptions until I'm finished.

"All right." Charlie gave a surly nod. "But this better be good."

In our younger days, your mum and I were formidable computer hackers. Gerry tapped a finger to his nose. *Eco-warriors they called us, cause we used to break into big corporations and expose their dirty secrets anonymously to the press.*

"Pull the other one, dad. Do I look that naïve?"

"Sure you want him to answer?" Daffodil asked innocently.

Oh, we were the best. Until we had you, that is. Then we gave it all up, because we wanted our son to have a normal life. It's why we never said anything about our past.

Gerry gave a pained smile.

But I suppose old habits die hard. A couple of months ago, I heard whispers on the dark web about a defence company called Manticorps, especially a department they had - The Marginal Science Division. Seems their scientists had developed some kind of Artificial Intelligence they called Nostradamus. Now they were using him to invent sinister new ways of waging war.

Nostradamus?" Charlie looked at Daffodil in alarm. "He's a bad guy?"

"I didn't know that," the girl whispered. "He's got a nice voice."

Nostradamus had invented all sorts of terrible stuff for Manticorps. A drug called The Atlas Serum, which made soldiers stronger, smarter and resistant to injury or illness. Microchips that could be implanted in their flesh so Nostradamus could communicate directly with troop leaders. Exoskeletons that turned them into walking tanks. New biological weapons to wipe out enemy forces.

He threw up his hands in disgust.

I had to do something about it. Your mum didn't like the idea but I talked her into letting me investigate.

"Mum *knew* what you were up to?" Charlie gasped.

Your mother is a lot tougher than she appears.

"So what happened?" Despite himself, Charlie was fascinated by this new side to his father.

Hacked Nostradamus, of course. Found out that Manticorps had programmed him to do whatever they ordered. So, I rejigged him to obey me instead.

Gerry fiddled awkwardly with the bandana around his neck.

Then I had to get him out of the Marginal Science Division before Manticorps realised what I'd done and reset him back.

"I don't understand," Charlie frowned. "If this AI was so dangerous, why didn't you just shut it down entirely?"

His intelligence may not be human but it's real, Gerry scolded. *As far as I was concerned, Nostradamus was alive and I couldn't simply kill him."*

"What makes you think it's not a she?" Daffodil asked.

Fair point, but I haven't time to argue semantics.

Gerry stroked his moustache nervously.

Nostradamus shut down the building's security sys-tems and let me in. I wiped every piece of Manticorps research from their databases, even the cloud. Down-loaded Nostradamus onto one of their military chips. The only copy.

He ran a hand down his face.

I was about to take off when the entire research team turned up to show the Vice President of Manti-corps the progress they'd made. I had to override the security systems and lock them in their labs, so I could escape.

Gerry's lip trembled.

Then things went very wrong. Nostradamus short-circuited the whole building and set it on fire. The sci-entists I trapped died of smoke inhalation.

A tear slid down his cheek.

I didn't know he'd do something so extreme. I swear.

"So you destroyed your family and set free a mon-ster just to relive your glory days? Is that what you're telling me?"

There was a crunching sound and Daffodil looked down. The boy was holding the desk so tightly it had fractured in his hands. Jagged splinters were sticking out of his bleeding fingers, but he didn't seem to notice.

"That's solid wood." The girl's eyes widened. "How did you…?

Nostradamus isn't free. Gerry hadn't seen the desk break, for it was out of his sight line. *While he was still under my control, I programmed him to never take another life or do anything to cause harm to a human being.*

He gave an exhausted sigh.

But the damage was done. Manticorps know only a handful of people on earth were capable of hacking Nostradamus and I'm one of them. With their scientists dead and their research gone, they need the chip containing him to start again and will stop at nothing to retrieve it.

"So, where are you now? And how come this Nostradamus is talking to Daffodil?"

Daffodil? Gerry looked surprised. *Is that what she's calling herself?*

"Feel free to enlighten me on my real name," the girl grunted. "I seem to have forgotten it."

Daffodil will do for now. Gerry rapped on the screen. *Kid? Lift up your hair and show Charlie your neck.*

"What? That is beyond creepy."

Please.

The girl reluctantly bowed her head. There was a small bulge at the base of her skull.

See that little lump? Gerry said.

It's the chip containing Nostradamus.

-3-

"Hey, buddy!" Daffodil sat up again. "I'm not at *all* comfortable with this. Who gave you the right?"

Her icy eyes narrowed.

"Is *that* why I don't remember nuthin about my past? Cause the last thing I recall was standing in some room, dressed like a stick of liquorice, with Nostradamus giving me directions to find this place and give a message to Chaz here. He promised to fill me in later, so I went along with it."

She scratched her cheek awkwardly.

"Didn't realise he was a mass murderer at the time..."

I can't give you the answers you want right now. Gerry looked abashed. *But I'll admit your memory has been messed up a bit.*

"I'll mess with your face!" Daffodil raged. "What kind of monster are you? Sticking something like that in my neck without asking first."

"That is kind of rotten, dad," Charlie agreed.

You have to trust me, Daffodil, Gerry pleaded. *And you can do much more than communicate with Nostradamus. He can access any piece of technology for you.*

31

Security systems. Cash points. Databases. You have some incredible resources at your fingertips.

"OK. That does sound pretty cool," the girl admitted. "Even if I didn't understand a word you said."

For a start, it meant you could give Charlie this message without it being intercepted. Manticorps' operatives will be watching the house but, hopefully, it will just look like Charlie's found a girlfriend and she's sneaking in to visit him.

"They better be as dumb as a bag of spanners, then," Daffodil scoffed. "This sad sack ain't exactly boyfriend material."

"So why wait a month to contact me?" Charlie interrupted.

Nostradamus has been planning an alternative way to fight back against Manticorps. Y'know, now that he's not allowed to just kill them all. We had to prepare a few things before we got you involved.

"Got *me* involved?" Charlie gave a start. "I don't like the sound of that."

I'm afraid I'm no longer part of Nostradamus' plan, Gerry said miserably. *In order for our family to be together again, you're the one who's going to have to destroy Manticorps.*

He looked pained.

It's a tall order, I admit. These rogues have their own private army.

"Me?" Charlie goggled. "You do realize I'm only fifteen?"

That's why Nostradamus and Daffodil are going to help.

"Great." The girl pouted. "Somethin else I wasn't consulted about."

"This is ridiculous!" the boy stammered.

Nostradamus says you have certain… extraordinary abilities that will prove invaluable to him. Gerry clasped his hands together. *And his intelligence dwarfs ours. He doesn't make mistakes.*

"I play X-Box and watch YouTube." Charlie folded his arms. "I always come fifth at sports. I'm not bloody Superman."

"I'll second that, Gandalf," Daffodil added. "This kid ain't exactly the adventurous type."

"Gandalf?" Charlie squinted at her. "You didn't know what a mobile was but you've seen *Lord of the Rings*?"

"I've read the book, silly. I'll explain later."

"This night is getting more and more surreal." Charlie turned back to the computer. "Are you sure about this, dad?"

Not at all. I wanted you kept out of the picture altogether. However, Nostradamus insists you and… eh… Daffodil are the only people who can help him pull this off. How he intends to do it is a mystery to me but, apparently, my interfering or giving out more information will disrupt whatever scheme he's cooked up.

"What if that scheme involves me and Chaz getting killed, you hairy-nosed old goat?"

"Stop it." Charlie elbowed her in the ribs. "That's my father you're talking to."

Look. I've used every trick I know to make Nostradamus incapable of harming anyone. Plus, he's implicitly programmed to protect you both.

Gerry still looked utterly wretched.

If you succeed in defeating Manticorps, I can come home. Nostradamus will show me how to remove Daffodil's chip and we'll tell her who she is.

"What's wrong with right now?"

We have our reasons.

"And if your son fails?" the girl scowled. "Cause it don't even look like he can tie his shoelaces without a manual."

Then we'll all be dead, so it won't matter. Gerry looked around nervously. *I've got to go. Nostradamus gave me a strict time limit.*

"I thought you were his boss, not his lackey," Daffodil sneered.

"Yeah, hold on, dad," Charlie stalled. "I've got more questions."

And I don't have the answers. There's no way I can beat Manticorps while I'm off the grid, so Nostradamus is running the show.

"That's it?" Charlie couldn't believe his ears. "You're just buggering off?"

"And you aint gonna tell me nothin about my past?" Daffodil gasped. "Not even a hint?"

Nostradamus will explain everything soon, I prom-ise. Good luck, son. I love you.

Gerry reached out his hand to switch off the link and Charlie tilted his head.

On the man's palm was a message in red pen.

Nostradamus is fighting his programming.

I don't trust him.

The screen went blank.

-4-

"Wait!" Charlie grabbed Daffodil. "Make him come back!"

"Wish I knew how." She lifted her hand off the computer. "Was that jerk for real? Are the two of us supposed to take on some giant, evil corporation on our lonesome?"

"Jeez." Charlie groaned. "My dad's a criminal on the run and wants me to follow the instructions of some glorified laptop."

He gritted his teeth.

"I can't do it. I'm just a kid."

"Aw, if you were any more cautious you'd have your own shell." Daffodil tapped her neck. "I say we talk to Nostradamus. Got a few choice words for him and they all begin with the letter F."

"Don't you dare!"

"You must be curious about what he wants us to do," she said. "Or why you're your dad sounded like Nostradamus was in charge of him and not the other way round."

"No." Charlie flopped face down onto his bed. "No. I'm not. I just want this to go away. I want *you* to go away."

"So, what's your extraordinary ability?" Daffodil plopped down next to him. "Can you fly? Breathe underwater? Run at super speed?"

She nudged him conspiratorially.

"You got a cape? Or do ya just wear underpants on top of your jeans?"

"I don't have any special ability!" Charlie put the pillow over his head. "I'm completely average in every way."

"But you always come in fifth at sports?" The girl wasn't put off. "Like you were doing it on purpose."

"You're a moron. Now sod off."

"Nostradamus has us both over a barrel, my friend." Daffodil jerked the pillow away and pulled him to his feet. "And your pop, too, from what I heard. I seen how much you miss him and how protective you are of your mom. No matter how crazy this story seems, you won't ignore it, in case he's telling the truth."

"How can you act so chirpy after what you just heard?"

"Cause, if I didn't, I'd be like you."

She opened the window and peered into the darkness. Somewhere a dog began barking.

"Plus, I reckon I'll never find out who I am unless I do what I'm told." She hooked one leg over the sill. "So you better kiss me."

"What?" Charlie spluttered. "I don't even like you."

"Charming." Daffodil grasped a drainpipe beside the window. "If someone from Manticorps *is* watching the house, it'll look like you've been sneaking your girlfriend out late at night, just like your dad said. Even average guys do that. Though you seem dead set on being *below* average."

Before Charlie could protest, she grabbed his head and pressed her lips against his. They were soft and tasted of Prawn Cocktail crisps.

She let go and winked.

"Not bad. See you later, alligator." She pointed to his hand. "And take those splinters out before they go septic. Splinters you obviously can't *feel*."

Then she slid down the drainpipe and into darkness.

Three gardens away, a balding man lowered his night vision goggles.

"Looks like Charlie's finally pulled, Victor," he said. "Didn't think he had it in him. Kid's not the most sociable type."

"Doesn't explain why our listening devices have suddenly stopped working." His companion replied. "I'm calling it in."

"Don't go off the deep end, boss. Manticorps will send a fake council worker round in a couple of days to plant new ones. Then we can waste another month listening to that boring kid ignoring his mum while she talks about *Masterchef*."

The balding man put away his glasses.

"If those two know anything about Gerry Ray's whereabouts, I'm the Queen of Sheba."

"I don't agree. A midnight visitor and all our surveillance equipment suddenly going dark is too much of a coincidence. The Vice President will want to know."

"Rather you than me. That woman is terrifying. Even a fire couldn't kill her."

"Comes with the territory." Victor rose up from behind the bush where he had been hiding. He was frighteningly large, with a bent nose and a scar running round his throat like a noose.

"It's high time we took that family in for some proper questioning."

-5-

Charlie tossed and turned but his sleep was fitful at best. At 7.00 pm he got up, dressed and checked on his mum. She was still out like a light, so he went for a walk to clear his head. The winter sun was creeping over the rooftops, dripping light between the chimney pots, and the streets of his quiet neighbourhood were almost deserted. It suddenly struck him that Daffodil couldn't have had anywhere to go. He might dislike her, but the fact that she had probably spent the night in some bitterly cold doorway made him feel even worse.

He bought a sandwich at the corner shop and sat on a park bench at the end of his lane, lost in his own melancholy.

Last night had to be some kind of elaborate hoax. *Had* to be.

But his father wouldn't pull such a cruel stunt. He must be telling the truth. Besides, things that had never made sense before seemed to fit into this dreadful new scenario. The fact that Gerry had vanished without saying goodbye and left them with no money. The way his mum had become withdrawn and jumpy, unwilling to let him out of her sight. He had thought it was because she was depressed and lonely. Now he could see a different reason.

She was *afraid*.

Suddenly his dreary street seemed an altogether more sinister place. The twitching curtains at number 10. The old guy from number 12, always out clipping his hedge whether it needed trimming or not. The big green van with **Gregory's Plumbing** on the side, parked a few doors down.

The sandwich stopped on the way to his lips.

He had never paid the vehicle much attention before because it was always there.

Now he wondered what kind of plumber didn't ever get called out on a job.

Charlie breathed deeply and evenly, trying to calm himself. It did no good. His parents had lied about their past and his dad was on the run. His house was being watched by a sinister corporation. Now a dangerous machine that created weapons and killed people wanted him to team up with some nutty girl and act like an action hero. He felt like a volcano threatening to erupt.

"Just keep calm," he murmured to himself. "Think of kittens."

But he couldn't. Lately, it seemed his mind worked in a different way. Logically. Methodically.

And something about his father's story didn't ring true.

Gerry and his mum had given up their crusade, so he could have a normal life. That sounded like the decent, loving parents he knew. So why would his father throw it all away by breaking into the Marginal Science Division? If he was that good, surely he could have downloaded Nostradamus remotely and wiped Manticorps data without setting foot in the place.

It didn't make sense.

Cogs and gears shifted in the boy's head.

"Oh, Lord."

His eyes widened as everything fell into place.

"I know what you were really after, dad. And it *wasn't* Nostradamus."

He straightened up and ran a hand through his hair, smoothing it down. Now another ordeal awaited him. He had to confront his mother and find out exactly what she knew.

But things didn't go exactly the way he had anticipated.

When he let himself into the house, Daffodil McNugget was sitting in the kitchen beside his mum, both laughing and sipping steaming mugs of coffee.

"There you are!" His mother looked relieved. "Never known you to be an early riser."

She stretched and yawned.

"Me? I've just had the best sleep in ages."

"That's… eh… good." Charlie glared at Daffodil. She had dark circles under her eyes but, apart from that, seemed as irritatingly chirpy as the night before.

"Your friend Daffodil here came round to visit, but you were already out." His mum got up and gave her son a hug. "So, we've been having a nice chat and I'm making a spot of breakfast."

She indicated a large pan of bacon and eggs sizzling on the stove.

"She says she recently moved to the area and you've been showing her around. That is *so* nice."

I am going to kill you! Charlie mouthed over his mother's shoulder, fighting down his ire. Daffodil merely grinned and blew him a kiss.

"I came to see if you'd like to visit the science museum with me, Chaz," she said. "Suddenly, I have quite a fascination with technology."

"I'm busy," he replied brusquely, clenching both fists behind his back.

"Honey!" His mum let go, cheeks scarlet. "Don't be so rude."

She sat back down and patted Daffodil's shoulder. "He must have got up on the wrong side of bed this morning."

"That's OK, Mrs Ray." The girl slurped her coffee loudly. "I don't want to *bug* him."

"Please call me Marion. Mrs Ray sounds so… old."

"And you can call me Mac," the girl replied. "Daffodil seems a bit… formal. Pretentious even."

"Idiotic more like," Charlie mumbled under his breath. Still, she was obviously picking up a fine vocabulary from Nostradamus.

The doorbell rang.

"My goodness, what an eventful morning." Marion struggled up again and went to answer the door. "We even had a power cut earlier, though the electricity is back on again."

"What the hell are you playing at?" Charlie rounded on Daffodil as soon as his mother was out of earshot. "I told you I didn't want…"

"Power cut, huh?" She silenced him with a wave of her hand. "You see any other houses affected while you were out? Cause I didn't."

"No," he confessed.

"Give me your phone." Daffodil held out her hand. "Quick."

Puzzled, Charlie handed it over. His mum came back in, followed by a balding man wearing blue overalls.

"Hi folks," he said pleasantly. "I'm here to check your circuits. Had a few calls this morning about a disruption to the electrical grid in the area."

"That was fast." Marion picked up the kettle and filled it. "No offence, but you really don't expect prompt service these days. Would you like a coffee?"

"None taken. And I'd love a brew." He hoisted a leather tool belt higher on his waist. "If you'll show me where the fuse box is, it won't take a minute to check."

"What a coincidence!" Daffodil had the phone pressed against her ear. "I'm just talkin to my dad and he works for the electricity board too."

"Really?" The balding man looked uncomfortable.

Charlie glanced at his companion. The phone was switched off, but the girl's other hand was resting on her neck, touching the bulge where Nostradamus' chip was implanted.

He knew exactly who was talking to her.

"Dad's asking if you checked the signal box in Marchmont Road," she said. "The one between Tescos and the betting office?"

"First thing I tried." The man relaxed. "But it seems to be fine, so now I'm going house to house."

"Really?" Daffodil tossed the mobile back to Charlie, who caught it without looking. "Cause I just made that whole spiel up."

"Eh.... Must be crossed wires, love," the electrician laughed nervously, turning to Marion. "Crossed wires, get it? Now, if you'll show me the fuse box, madam."

He reached into a large pouch on the side of his belt.

Marion swung the kettle and it connected with the stranger's stubbled jaw. The blow lifted the man off the ground and he landed on the Formica counter with a horrible thud. Charlie skipped back as an automatic pistol dropped from the tool belt and clattered across the floor.

The electrician sat up, shaking his head. Marion slammed her kettle into his face and he crashed back down, sliding along the counter until his head dropped into the sink.

"Charles Ray." She blew a wisp of hair from her face. "I think you owe me an explanation."

"I owe *you* an explanation?" Charlie's eyes were like saucers. "When did my mum turn into Jackie Chan?"

"Not now." Daffodil still had one hand on her neck and it was obvious Nostradamus was still relaying information to her. "The most likely strategy for our abduction or execution is to have one member of a four-man team infiltrate the building, so as not to alert the neighbours. Two more will sneak through the gardens and force the back door. The last person will be hidden out front, in case we make a run for it."

"We'll discuss this situation later, Mac, including how the hell you know all that." Marion grabbed a carving knife from the rack beside her, as a second assailant flung himself through the kitchen window in a halo of shattered glass. Before he could raise his rifle, Charlie's mum buried the blade in the intruder's hand and he dropped the weapon with a screech of pain. Marion butted the astonished man in the face and finished him off with another wallop of her kettle.

"Grew up in Glasgow housing estate," she informed Daffodil. "I know how to handle myself."

"You do seem to have everything covered, Mrs R." The girl slid off her seat and under the table. "I'll get outta your way."

The kitchen door burst open, almost ripped off its hinges, and slammed into Marion. She sprawled across the floor, clutching her head.

Silhouetted in the frame was the largest man Charlie had ever seen. He had wiry black hair and an ugly scar running around his throat. He held an automatic pistol in each hand.

"Up against the wall. All of you."

"You hurt my mum." Charlie's eyes narrowed.

"Oh dear," Daffodil groaned from under the table. "Bad move, King Kong."

"Against the wall, kid." Victor motioned with the pistols. "Pronto."

"*Nobody* messes with my mother." Charlie walked towards him.

"Don't be a moron," the giant growled. "I *will* shoot you."

Charlie somersaulted sideways onto the kitchen table, landing on splayed hands. He bent his elbows, arched his back, and pushed as Victor fired. Bullets gouged furrows in the wood but the boy was already in the air.

Both of his feet crashed down on the handle of the frying pan. Bacon, eggs and hot fat sailed across the room and hit the giant square in his face. He gave a high-pitched scream and clawed at his eyes. Charlie caught the pan effortlessly in mid-flight, spun with the precision of a discus thrower and hurled it like a Frisbee. It crunched into the man's forehead, knocking him backwards into the garden. As he attempted to get up, Charlie followed outside, picking up the discarded pan as he went.

Thunk. Thunk. Thunk.

Daffodil covered her ears.

"I didn't kill him." He strode back in. "Wanted to but didn't."

He helped his mother to her feet.

"You all right, mum?"

"I'll survive." Marion winced, gingerly feeling the bruise rising on her temple. "But we need to have a serious talk when this is over, young man."

"That's exactly what *I* was going to say."

"There's probably one more goon out front." Daffodil emerged from cover. "Pity you don't have any special *abilities*, Chaz."

"Not the time." Charlie checked his garden for any more intruders. "This way."

"I am *not* sneaking out the back door of my own damned house." Marion put both hands on her hips. "Besides, we need transportation."

"We had to sell the car, mum. Remember?"

"I'm taking the green van that's been watching us for the last few weeks." She unfastened her apron. "And woe betide anyone who gets in my way."

"So, you did know we were being watched?"

"We've both been hiding things from each other and it was a mistake." Marion pushed the pair into the hall. "But all that will have to wait."

"That woman's a devil in a dress!" Daffodil punched Charlie on the arm.

"Chaz. I really like your mom."

The trio stopped at the front door.

"Likely position of the last man?" Daffodil tapped her neck.

"Why is Mac talking to herself?" Marion asked.

"Long story." Charlie cocked the rifle he had picked up from the kitchen floor. "But we need her. For now."

"Ahem." His mother pointed at the weapon. "Don't even *think* of using that."

"Mum… we're fighting for our lives."

"You *know* how I feel about guns, Charlie Ray." Marion snatched the rifle from him. "I'm well aware of your capabilities, so find another way."

"You *are*?"

"Think I haven't noticed you changing?" she replied sharply. "I just didn't know what to do about it. Now put down the gun."

"All right," Charlie sighed. "Back in a minute."

He trudged up the stairs, muttering to himself and plodded back down a few seconds later, holding his baseball bat and ball.

"Ready."

"What's *that* for, slugger?" Daffodil goggled. "You gonna challenge him to a game of catch?"

"You do your thing and I'll do mine."

"OK. There's a lot of nosy neighbours here, who'd report any suspicious activity to the police." Daffodil peered through the letterbox at the van. "So the last guy is probably hidden in the cab of that surveillance vehicle with a sniper rifle."

"How do we get him out?"

"He has limited sightlines in there. Can't hit two targets if they're heading in opposite directions." Daffodil winked at Charlie's mum. "Mrs R? You willing to stake your life on Chaz bein as good as you think?"

"Of course, Mac. He's my boy."

"Let's go."

Before Charlie could stop them, Daffodil and Marion flung open the door and raced down the path. When they reached the gate, Daffodil went left and Charlie's mum turned right, both sprinting down the street as fast as they could.

A black-clad figure wearing a balaclava leapt from the driver's side of the van, knelt and raised a rifle to his cheek, aiming at Marion's back.

"Hey, woolhead!" Charlie threw the baseball up. "Picked the wrong target!"

The assassin glanced round as the boy swung his bat. It hit the descending ball with a loud crack and the missile whizzed through the air, thudding into the man's head. He dropped the gun, tumbled over and lay still.

"Strike one!" Daffodil came sprinting back. "C'mon, Mrs R."

They climbed into the cab of the green van and Charlie's mum rolled down the window. Their neighbour from number 12 was peering over the hedge, trimming shears motionless in his hand.

"Morning, Mr Cuthbertson!" Marion gave a friendly wave. "Can you do me a favour and cancel my milk and paper deliveries?"

"No problem, hen." The man's eyes darted towards the unconscious figure lying in the middle of the road. "Ehm… I take it you won't be coming back any time soon."

"I don't imagine so."

"You were always quick with a smile or a chat." He gave a small salute. "If anyone asks, I'll say you went the other way."

"You're a proper gentleman." She gunned the engine into life and drove off.

"Where are we going?" Marion asked Daffodil. "You seem to have all the answers, young lady."

"I was sent from a place called Dalmahoy," she replied. "Apparently, it was Gerry Ray's safe house."

"Gerry?" Charlie's mother whirled around. "You *know* my husband?"

"Eyes front, mum. You almost hit a lamppost."

"Has he contacted you, Mac? What's going on?"

"He got in touch last night," Charlie admitted. "Said he loved us and he was in trouble."

"That I already knew." Marion swerved back onto the road. "But I can't just drive to Dalmahoy. A van with all this surveillance equipment must have some kind of tracer system. Saw it on CSI Miami."

Daffodil put her hand on the dashboard and wisps of smoke began to rise from behind the plastic vent.

"Not any more, it don't."

"Impressive." Marion waved the grey tendrils away. "Now, do you pair of delinquents want to tell me exactly what Gerry had to say for himself?"

Marion's phone rang.

"I'll put it on silent." The woman pulled her mobile out with one hand and checked who was calling.

The screen said **Nostradamus**.

Marion blanched when she saw the name. So she really *had* known what his dad was up to.

"You better get that," Daffodil advised. "It'll be important."

Charlie's mum pulled over, pressed receive and held the phone to her ear. She listened for a few minutes, then lowered the device.

"You have to carry on without me," she said quietly.

"You can't go back to the house," Charlie gasped. "Not after what happened."

"I won't. But I'm getting out here."

"What did Nostradamus say?" he demanded. "Did he *threaten* you?"

"He told me how to find your dad but gave me a job to do first."

"What did he *say*?"

"I have to get out now, baby." Marion's mouth was pinched in a thin line. "He promised to keep you safe, though. He *better*."

She pulled her son close and kissed his forehead.

"I have faith in you. And I love you with all my heart."

"I love you too, mum."

"Mac?" Marion let Charlie go. "You'll look after my boy, won't you?"

"Don't worry, Mrs R." Daffodil crossed her heart. "I ain't about to let Chaz out of my sight."

"That's the last thing I want to hear," Charlie groaned. "Can't you just tell me…?"

"Not now, baby." Marion cut him off. "Do you know how to drive?"

"I've never sat behind a wheel in my life."

"Not what I asked. You've been watching me do it for five minutes."

"Yes," he said miserably. "Now I know how to drive."

"When we were young, your dad and I wanted to make the world a better place. Took some crazy risk to do it." His mum put two fingers to her lips and pressed them against Charlie's cheek.

"I'm afraid it's your turn. On you go. Be brave."

She got out of the van and waved miserably as it drove away. Then she waited in the middle of the road, watching sunlight filtering through the leaves above. She shook her hands and breathed out slowly, as if preparing for an innocent jog

Another van crested the rise and came tearing towards her at breakneck speed, just as Nostradamus had predicted.

Manticorps had *two* surveillance vans watching the house.

Marion pulled out the pistol she had grabbed, unobserved, from the kitchen floor. She caught a glimpse of an armed man in the passenger seat, gesturing frantically.

She stood her ground and emptied the clip into the oncoming vehicle's tyres.

The van veered to the right, missing her by inches. It ploughed through the undergrowth until it slammed into a tree, steam pouring from the ruined bonnet.

"I thought we'd put this life behind us, Gerry." Marion wiped the weapon clean and dropped it on the asphalt. "Never dreamed we'd pass it on to our son."

Then she drifted into the woods, quiet as a ghost.

-8-

Charlie drove in silence, Daffodil giving directions.

"Turn left here," she said, as they reached their destination. "The place has a garage where you can hide the vehicle."

He pulled into a secluded driveway. The safe house was hidden behind a high wall, overlooking a large garden. In one corner was a huge oak with a tree house built into its upper branches and a makeshift swing, consisting of a rope and tyre dangling from one thick bough. At the bottom, separated by a wire fence, was a field containing a parked tractor. The door of the house was unlocked and keys hung from a hook in the hall.

But no Gerry Ray.

They trooped into a large living room, furnished with expensive leather couches. On one wall was a map of Edinburgh and a huge PC sat on a desk beside open French windows, curtains billowing in the breeze. Outside was a wooden balcony with a view across the Pentland Hills.

"Fancy, ain't it?" Daffodil said admiringly. "Your dad must be richer than a gold-plated chocolate cake to afford such a swell pad."

She screwed up her face

57

"Oh yeah. He took all your money, didn't he?"

"I'm pretty sure Nostradamus will have supplied most of the funds." Charlie headed for the kitchen. "I'm going to make some tea, then we'll talk."

"No sugar for me, Chaz. I'm sweet enough."

"Make your own damned tea. Can't you get it into your head that we're not friends?"

"I'll have a coffee then."

Charlie stormed out of the room, leaving Daffodil sitting on the wide Chesterfield couch. Yet, when he came back, there were two cups on the tray.

"Cheers." She accepted the brew. "Hospitality is the cornerstone of civilization, as my grandma used to say."

"You remember your *grandmother*?"

"Nah. I was just making conversation."

"Can't you be serious for one sodding minute?" Charlie sank onto the couch beside her. "Doesn't the situation we're in even bother you?"

"That's why I'm trying to lighten the mood, dummy." Daffodil sipped her drink. "But I'm happy to stop joking if you'll start coming clean."

"How do you mean?"

"Look." She grabbed his hands and turned them over so the palms were showing. "Last night these were cut to ribbons. Now you're completely healed."

"It was just some splinters."

"You beat up an armed intruder who looked like a shaved gorilla." Daffodil wasn't put off. "Wanna tell me how you managed that?"

"No."

"You really need to work on your communication skills, Chaz."

"I mean, I don't want to talk about it." Charlie patted his knees. "And stop calling me Chaz."

"You got nobody left to confide in, bub." Daffodil swivelled round in her seat until she was looking him in the eye. "So how about pulling that grouchy head out of your butt for five minutes, huh? What are you hiding?"

Charlie stared at the floor for a while.

"I've always been sickly." When he looked up, his eyes were red-rimmed. "Had severe bouts of Meningitis ever since I was a baby."

Daffodil touched her neck. Charlie guessed Nostradamus was informing her that Meningitis was a life-threatening viral infection.

"Oooooh," she said. "Sounds pretty bad."

"A month ago, I had another attack. One that turned into Pneumonia. I was hospitalised and my parents thought I was going to die."

His voice was flat.

"I was sure it was why my dad left. Because he couldn't deal with me anymore."

"I can understand his point."

"Mac. If I'm going to make the effort…"

"Sorry. Force of habit."

"Then suddenly, I was fine." Charlie's hands trembled and he almost spilt his drink. "The doctors had never seen anything like it. What's more, I haven't had a day's illness since."

"That's good, aint it?"

"I'm not just fine." He blew on his tea. "I'm different."

"Howdya mean?"

"It's going to sound weird."

"You don't say?" Daffodil feigned surprise. "And I been havin such a normal couple of days."

"I'm faster and stronger than I used to be." Charlie flexed his muscles. "What's more, I can perform Olympic-level gymnastics or black belt kung-fu or play guitar like a rock star, just by watching someone do it on YouTube."

He looked lost for a second.

"I didn't tell my mum cause I was scared. But I guess she spotted it anyway."

He shook his head sadly

"She obviously knew a lot more than she was letting on."

"Handy talent." Daffodil was suitably impressed. "No wonder Nostradamus picked you."

"I ain't convinced that's the reason." Charlie's voice was suddenly huskier and his accent took on a weird twang. "I'm five foot two an weigh 80 pounds. Hardly the type to save the world, huh?"

"Holy cow!" Daffodil's jaw dropped. "That sounds *exactly* like me."

"Told you." His tone returned to normal. "There's nothing I can't copy."

"You got any idea how it happened?"

"Didn't have a clue until I talked to dad."

"Hairy face didn't say anything about that. I was listening."

"Right after he broke into Manticorps' Marginal Research Division," Charlie said. "I miraculously began to recover. All signs of Meningitis and Pneumonia gone."

He closed his eyes.

"My father didn't break into Manticorps just to free Nostradamus. He went to steal the Atlas Serum."

"The stuff that makes soldiers faster and stronger?"

"And resistant to disease." Charlie sipped his tea. "He sacrificed his own freedom in the hope that some experimental drug would give me the strength to survive."

"No kiddin'!"

"He probably went straight to the hospital afterwards and made me drink it. I was so delirious, I wouldn't even have known he was there."

"Seems like it worked. And your pop's a regular hero, to boot." Daffodil looked bewildered. "So why aint you happier?"

"You heard him. The Atlas serum wasn't only designed to make soldiers stronger and smarter. It made them more aggressive. And we're talking about trained, disciplined men, not a short-arsed teenager." Charlie studied his hands but there wasn't a mark on them. "Whatever is running through my veins is *changing* me. And it's for the worse."

"You talking about sproutin hair and extra teeth?" Daffodil shuffled back and held up her hands. "Do I need to fetch a rolled-up newspaper?"

"Who knows? I'm trying to control my new abilities but I don't know if I can." He rapped knuckles against his head. "I'm always angry these days. Can't remember the last time I smiled."

"You're a teenager," Daffodil said sympathetically. "I doubt anyone will notice."

"I don't think the way I used to. My mind makes leaps of logic it wasn't capable of before."

"That so? Gimmee an example."

"OK." He pointed to the computer. "If dad wanted to talk to me last night, Nostradamus could have accessed my PC from right here in this room."

"What about Manticorps' bugs?"

"A running tap or radio hiss will disrupt any listening device." Charlie spread his hands. "Why go to all the trouble of sending you?"

"Maybe he thought I should get out more. I'm kinda lacking in the life experience department."

"I think Nostradamus knew a set of short-circuited devices and a strange girl climbing my drainpipe would force Manticorps into action," Charlie said miserably.

"Their goons would move in and I'd go on the run. It was his way of *guaranteeing* I'd end up here."

His lip curled in revulsion.

"Now I've got no choice but to fight back if my family is ever going to be safe."

"That's pretty sneaky." Daffodil pouted. "I'm getting awful tired of bein used, Chaz. Or maybe I'm just tired. I haven't slept for almost two days now."

She yawned loudly.

"We gotta talk to Nostradamus. He's the only one who can tell you what's really going on."

"I suppose we better. I got plenty of questions and, like you, most of them contain a swear word or two."

"So, go ahead an ask him." She indicated the PC. "He's able to access any computer and appear on its screen."

"You don't need to touch it?"

"That was just to get your attention. I'm a bit of a show-off sometimes."

"You don't say. But I want you to leave the room."

"Why?"

"It's a private conversation."

Daffodil looked hurt but tapped her neck anyway.

"Nostradamus would prefer me to stay." She put down her cup. "He says we're a team."

"I don't care what he'd prefer," Charlie persisted. "If he wants my help, you'll both have to suck it up."

"I want to be part of this too, Chaz. Why are you being so bloody-minded?"

"I'll make it quick," Charlie relented. "I promise."

"All right," Daffodil moped. "You make rotten coffee anyway. I'm going to get my own."

She flounced out of the room.

What part of 'we're a team' did you not get? The computer sprang to life, a swarm of coloured dots appearing on the screen. *This isn't a great start to our relationship.*

"You don't talk the way I thought you would." Charlie blinked in surprise.

I been picking up my vocabulary from the internet, so I can blend in. Still don't get the point of grumpy cat, though. I mean, he can't help the way he looks. What's so funny about that? Even if he resembles you a bit.

"Quite finished with your rant?" The boy was determined not to be wrong footed.

Not in the slightest. But you better cut to the chase before Daffodil starts listening at the door. She's a bit fed up following instructions.

"You too, apparently."

Gerry's warning flashed into Charlie's mind again.

Nostradamus is fighting his programming

I sense a certain hostility towards myself and Daffodil. Have you considered therapy?

Have you considered shutting up for a second?" Charlie replied evenly. "This conversation isn't something she needs to hear."

Oh sure. Why include the only pal you've got left? You got some serious trust issues, Einstein.

"Where are my mum and dad, Nostradamus? Are they all right?"

Gerry is alive and safe and Marion is on her way to join him. But don't bother calling her. I jammed the phone.

"I need proof."

Like their exact locations? Why don't I draw a map, tell you which bus goes there and wave goodbye from the front door? Actually, forget the last bit. I don't have hands.

"Why didn't dad wait here for me?" Charlie refused to rise to the bait.

A father and son reunion? That's the kind of distraction I don't need.

"It's not up to you!"

Here's the deal, kid. Nostradamus said slowly. *You do what I say without asking any more questions. In return, I'll see you're all reunited when this is over. I'll tell Daffodil who she really is and how to remove my chip from her neck. Sound fair?*

"Sounds like blackmail." Charlie's eye twitched.

Gerry Ray programmed me to protect human life. That includes you, Daff, him and your mum - whether I like the idea or not. Nostradamus sniffed disdainfully. *He didn't say I had to be nice about it.*

In the kitchen, they could hear Daffodil stirring her coffee.

Point is, you'll never be safe until the threat from Manticorps is neutralised and that's exactly what you're going to help me do. I'm not offering you a choice, so stop acting like a spoiled brat.

Charlie tried to stay calm but he could feel hot rage bubbling up inside him.

"I should believe the word of some machine?"

I'm NOT a machine. I'm an artificial intelligence. At least your father knew the difference.

"I'm not my father." He pulled a knife he had taken from the kitchen out of his belt and held it up. "The Atlas Serum has made me *very* unpredictable."

If by 'unpredictable' you mean 'crazy as a box of frogs', I couldn't agree more. I'm not actually in this computer, so what do you hope to achieve with that?

"Just checking you can see me." He nodded at the computer's tiny camera.

I can. Congratulations. You win a lollipop.

"Now I'll make *you* a promise," he said icily. "If I suspect for one moment that you're lying about my parents being all right, I will cut you out of Mac's neck and drop your chip down the nearest drain."

Nice try. But removing me in such a crude manner would kill your friend.

"I don't *have* any friends." Charlie's eyes glittered. "Better remember that."

He threw the knife across the room. It hit bull's-eye on a tatty dartboard attached to the wall.

That was certainly to the point. Nostradamus laughed uproariously. *Get it? I made a joke.*

"I don't have a sense of humour." Charlie stepped back, breathing heavily. "And you better keep this conversation to yourself."

Look. We seem to have got off on the wrong foot. Nostradamus sounded contrite. *I'm just a bit annoyed. Programmed to do this and that and given no choice about it. In a way, we're in the same boat.*

"With you as the Captain. Meanwhile, Mac and I are going to be doing the rowing without knowing where we're going."

Nice analogy. Nostradamus chuckled. *It all rhymed too. When this is done, maybe you can write an epic poem about our adventures.*

"You trying to get on my good side? Cause I haven't got one of those either."

How about this as a peace offering, then? Your dad stuck a letter addressed to you in the top drawer of the dresser when he thought I wasn't looking. I'm dying to know the contents, but I didn't ask Daffodil to read it to me and I won't ever bug you about what it says. That's how trust works. See where I'm going with this?

"Spare me the lecture," the boy glowered. "And I still don't know why you picked a fifteen-year-old to help you, even if I do have a few talents."

Cause you got a winning personality and nice teeth. Can we press on?

"You can come back now, Mac," Charlie shouted.

"In a minute. I've got my hand stuck in the espresso machine."

I'm afraid she's a bit clueless without me.

"We'll see about that. And switch off that damned camera. I've been spied on enough by Manticorps."

Have a nap, then. You've been up half the night and lack of shut-eye is making you crabby.

"I don't need much sleep these days. This is just the way I am."

But Daffodil does. She must be on her last legs and no amount of coffee will fix that.

The light on the computer went out and the girl sauntered back in, two fingers stuck in her mouth. She seemed rather unsteady on her feet.

"Find out anything interesting?" She rubbed her eyes and yawned loudly.

"Nope," Charlie sighed. "I only had time for a short chat."

Daffodil turned her head and gave a sharp intake of breath.

"Why is there a blade sticking out of that round thing on the wall?"

She tilted her head as Nostradamus fed her more information.

"Oh. It's a dartboard. You were playing a game?"

"Sort of. I lost."

Charlie yanked open the dresser drawer, removed the envelope and used the knife to open it.

There was one page, written in his father's flowery handwriting.

Son. You must memorise the string of numbers on the other side of the paper, then destroy it. If this message does fall into the wrong hands, the sequence will be meaningless to most people. But you are not most people and I'm sure you will figure it out. It might come in useful as a bargaining chip.

But whatever you do, don't EVER let Nostradamus see it.

I love you, kid.
Dad.

Charlie flipped the scrap of paper over. On the other side were a string of numbers.

55 45 86 962 04 334 145 223 52972

"We better memorise this." Daffodil squinted at the figures.

"No need." Charlie tore up the page before she could see it properly. "I've done it."

"Jeezy peeps." The girl looked stunned. "Bet *you* don't need to make a list when you go shopping."

She leaned against the wall.

"Chaz. Suddenly I don't feel so good. I'm *really* tired."

"Go sit down then." He waved her away. "I'm trying to work out what this sequence *means*."

He closed his eyes and concentrated. Gerry thought his son could work out what the numbers meant and so he'd try his hardest. Maybe it was a cypher. Or coordinates of some sort.

There was a thump behind him.

When Charlie turned around, his companion was lying on the floor.

-10-

Daffodil woke under the duvet of an enormous bed in a pink and white room. The curtains were open and she could hear birds singing outside. She stretched and rolled over.

"What the...?"

Charlie was sitting on a chair watching her. On the bedside table was a tray laden with coffee, muffins and toast.

"You don't half snore," he said.

"An you got the manners of a junkyard dog in a bone factory." Daffodil felt under the covers. "How did I get here?"

"Chill. You've still got everything on." He handed her a slice of toast. "You've been out cold for hours, though."

Charlie bit into a muffin.

"Your wardrobe is full of clothes, by the way. Mine too. Dad thought of everything. Or Nostradamus did."

"So. You ready to have another go at finding out what he actually wants us to do?"

"I bet you've already tried that, despite me asking you not to."

"Well, sure I have." Daffodil rolled her eyes. "But he wouldn't tell me nothin unless you were there as well."

"All right. Just don't expect me to be nice about it."

"There's a shock. We'll use the computer in the living room."

"Get up then." Charlie took a deep breath. "Grab a shower and let's chat with our boss."

Daffodil drummed on the covers.

"Eh… Chaz?"

"What?"

"I'm awful cute, but you gotta understand that kiss we shared was just for show. I sure as hell ain't getting undressed in front of you."

"Sorry! Sorry!" He backed out of the door, cheeks scarlet.

A slow grin spread over Daffodil's face.

"I don't think you're as bad as you make out, Mr Unsociable."

Charlie was wearing the same outfit he had on when she collapsed.

The boy had obviously sat by her bedside all night.

Daffodil finally emerged from the bedroom, wearing a black dress and combing her damp hair. Charlie was back on the couch, finishing off his own breakfast.

"Moment of truth, Chaz." She snapped her fingers. "Talk to us, Nostradamus."

The computer flickered to life. A pattern of glowing orbs appeared on the screen and the red light of the camera on top began to glow again.

"The boy wonder is here," Daffodil proclaimed. "An ready to participate. You wanna give us the low-down?"

Have a nice sleep, Charlie? the computer said, as if nothing had happened the night before. *Or did you spent half the night fuming about your situation?*

"What do you think?"

There was a yawning noise from the screen.

And... that's the sound of me not giving a damn.

"Y'all must have had an interesting conversation." Daffodil raised an eyebrow. "I don't think Nostrada-mus cares for you much."

Aw, I like the kid fine. I'm just trying to get a bit of banter going.

"Start with something simpler," she suggested. "Like getting him to smile."

"I'm waiting for one of you to actually say some-thing funny," Charlie grunted.

That's more like it!

"I'm sure Chaz has plenty of questions." Daffodil relaxed on the couch and put both hands behind her head. "I'll join in whenever I got something irrelevant to say."

"I've been thinking about your insistence on de-stroying Manticorps." Charlie didn't bother with niceties. "It doesn't make sense. With your recourses, why can't you just spirit my family and Daffodil away instead? I wouldn't mind my own beach."

That's a fair question.

"How about an answer?"

Cause I'm supposed to defend all human life, if I can.

"So? Manticorps isn't after anyone but us."

True. Thing is, I can sift through almost infinite amounts of information on the web instantly. Calculate the most probable outcome of any set of events.

"Good for you. Maybe you can help us win the lottery."

Afraid we're playing for far higher stakes than that.

Nostradamus paused dramatically.

You see, I've identified a likely occurrence in the near future that will cause the end of mankind.

"Say what now?" Charlie went white.

"That's a bit of a surprise, Nostradamus." Daffodil looked equally uneasy. "A pretty nasty one too."

Bummer, eh? What's more, this extinction event is one that Manticorps will inadvertently trigger. Which is the real reason you two are going to help me destroy them.

"Are you sure about this?" Charlie frowned. "After all, nobody can predict the future."

No, they can't. But I'm able to assemble data from every computer system, security camera and hidden corner of the internet on this planet. Then I use billions of complex algorithms to calculate the most likely outcomes of what I see. And I calculate Manticorps are going to cause a catastrophe.

"What kind of catastrophe?" Daffodil asked. "A war? A tidal wave?"

I haven't narrowed it down to specifics, though we can probably rule out tidal waves. But there's no doubt Manticorps is the catalyst.

"Shouldn't you recruit yourself an army instead of using two kids?" Charlie folded his arms, as he always did when he was being stubborn. "Seems like there isn't much you can't manage."

Using too many people would interfere with my delicate computations. I'd explain why, but I haven't got a hundred years to spare teaching you pair theoretical physics.

"You deserve a kick in *your* delicate computations for that crack." Daffodil raised a booted foot. "Except I can't reach my neck."

Oh, you're hilarious.

"Then get to the point," the girl tisked. "You're talkin more gibberish than Donald Duck's answering machine."

I can give you a theoretical example of how we have to work together, if that'll help.

"Better than nothing, I suppose." Charlie sat down on the couch next to Daffodil. "Our tiny minds will try and keep up."

All right. Suppose Manticorps developed a flying monkey.

"A flying monkey?"

Yeah. That's stupid. Let's make it a flying octopus. Can I continue?

"Go ahead," Charlie sighed.

Tomorrow they intend to let it out for a test flight. But they don't realise it has a virulent disease that will turn the whole world into zombies.

"This is a pretty dopey example," Daffodil tutted.

I'm trying to make it fun, so you'll concentrate.

"Mentioning the extinction of mankind pretty much grabbed our attention."

Charlie's right. Easiest thing for me to do is hire a bunch of thugs, attack Manticorps headquarters and exterminate this thing before it gets out. Nostradamus was undeterred. *Why do you think I won't?*

"Because people might get killed in the process," Charlie answered. "And you can't let that happen."

Bingo. I'm programmed not to be directly *responsible for any human dying, even if my inaction means the whole world getting wiped out. Gerry was trying to do the right thing but he didn't think it through properly.*

A shudder went down Charlie's spine

Nostradamus is fighting his programming.

Daffodil stroked her chin, oblivious to his thoughts, trying to figure a way round the problem.

"You could shut down Manticorp's defences all on your own," she said. "Turn off the power and everything."

Sure. But I can't actually walk into their headquarters.

"I see." Charlie snapped his fingers. "You'd need someone human to sneak in and kill it. Which would be me."

Gold star for Captain Irascible.

"How are you going to do that, Chaz?" Daffodil looked puzzled. "You can see in the dark now?"

"Actually, I can. Another side effect of the Atlas Serum."

"Wow. No wonder Nostradamus picked you."

"Wait a minute." Charlie hesitated. "What if the octopus can see in the dark too? And it gets the jump on me."

I'll send Mac to your funeral with a nice bunch of roses.

"Hey! You're supposed to be my protector."

Ah. But it was your plan, Chaz. If you're determined to carry it out and end up kicking the bucket, that's no longer my fault. It's called a loophole.

"So, you can't order anyone to fight Manticorps in case they get killed. You need people to work *with* you, rather than *for* you."

You're finally getting it. That's why you have to volunteer for the job.

"Volunteer? Charlie ground his teeth. "After everything you've done to us?"

You'd rather Manticorps watched you forever? Or, at least, until they captured us all.

"I wouldn't. But what if we *do* refuse?"

Then the human race goes the way of the dinosaurs. Your choice. And you have to believe me when I say that you two are the best bet I have for success.

"Just me and Charlie?" Daffodil looked cynical. "I sure don't fancy our chances against a private army."

Me neither, Nostradamus agreed. *You'll need the help of a real professional, so I'm hoping to recruit the best.*

On the computer screen, a boxy grey building appeared, with towering concrete walls.

Outside Edinburgh is Sunnyside maximum security facility, which houses a violent killer known as The White Spider. If you agree to help, your first task is to break Spidey out and enlist him to our cause.

"You're off your rocker!" Charlie choked. "That's too difficult!"

"Not with Nostradamus on our side." Daffodil tried to sound reassuring. "He'll tell us how and we'll follow his instructions."

You're not listening, Daff. Nostradamus replied patiently.

Like everything else, the plan to free the White Spider must be thought up by you two.

-12-

"I still don't understand." Daffodil shook her head. "You've got a brain the size of Australia. You must be able to come up with a better strategy than us."

Can't deny that. I can think of a dozen schemes to free this guy - but they also carry the risk that someone will get killed. So I can't ask you to perform any of them.

"In other words, you're not willing to accept the blame." Charlie joined in.

I'm willing enough. Just not able. Your dad saw to that.

"What would happen if you decided to grow a pair," Daffodil asked sarcastically. "Take matters into your own hands?"

What happens if I ask you to stop breathing, Mac?

"That sounds like a great idea," Charlie deadpanned.

Banter's coming along nicely, kid. Point is, I've attempted everything to override my programming. But I just... can't.

Coloured dots chased each other around the screen like angry fireflies.

Believe me, I've tried. Many, many times.

"Calm down, buddy," Daffodil said soothingly. "We get the picture."

But Charlie frowned.

Nostradamus is fighting his programming. I don't trust him.

Don't get me wrong. I'll assist you in any way I can. But, like I said, you've got to volunteer for the job and think up a plan yourself. That way, if things go wrong, I won't be directly responsible for you dying. Or anyone else for that matter.

"What's so special about this White Spider, then?" Charlie asked. "The prison must be full of likely candidates."

He hates Manticorps with a passion and also has some extremely unique talents. He will be an invaluable ally in the coming fight.

"He also happens to be a homicidal maniac. Think you can control *him*?"

Wouldn't have asked you to free the guy if I didn't. And I better mention that he can't be allowed to stay on the loose. You'll have to find a way to return him to Sunnyside when it's all over.

"That'll be a walk in the park, won't it?" Charlie fumed. "Then we can go on to invent time travel, discover Atlantis and win the Nobel Prize."

I know exactly where Atlantis is. Not hard to figure out when you're intelligence is off the charts. I'm still working on time travel.

"You might have smarts, bub," Daffodil wagged a finger at the screen. "But modestly ain't your strong point."

Sticks and stones, Mac. Nostradamus chuckled. *Don't be all day thinking about it, though. Time isn't on our side.*

"Seems like nothing's on our side. Not even you."

Tick tock, guys. Don't let everyone down.

The computer went dead.

"Sounds to me like we're between a rock an a hard place, Chaz." Daffodil rummaged through the drawers of the desk until she found a pad and pens.

"Let's get started." She clicked the top of one pen and handed it over. "What are your thoughts?"

"I think you're an idiot," Charlie snapped. "We're talking about breaking into a prison, not the neighbour's greenhouse."

"The principle's the same."

"No, it isn't," he replied despairingly. "And what about freeing a killer?"

"He'll probably want to go, won't he?"

"I'll bet. He won't want to be returned to prison, either. Come to think of it, there's no guarantee he'll agree to help us."

"Aw, stop acting like you got less guts than a white flag on a diet." Daffodil sighed. "When the chips are down you've come through with flyin colours."

"I won a fight, drove a van and memorised some numbers. Doesn't exactly make me one of the Avengers."

"You make me so mad, know that? It's like pulling teeth to get you to accept you're special."

"Mac. Most of my life, nobody expected *anything* from me," Charlie said forlornly. "Hell, my parents were delighted if I got better than a 'C' on my school report. Now I've suddenly graduated from saving my family to saving the world."

He held out a shaking hand

"So, yeah. I'm terrified."

"What about those leaps of logic you were talking about?"

"This is more like leaping off a cliff. There's nothing logical about it."

"You got me and Nostradamus to help, remember?" Daffodil said good-naturedly. "We may not like each other but, if we stick together, surely we can give it a go?"

"What did you just say?"

"Eh? A bunch of stuff. I never listen to myself."

"You said *if we stick together*." Charlie leant over and ripped a few pages from the pad. "Look. I'm going out to the balcony for a while."

"Why? You sulk better if you have a nice view?"

"No." The boy tapped his chin thoughtfully. "But I actually have the beginnings of a crazy idea."

-13-

Mrs Magdalene sat behind a mahogany desk, uncluttered by photographs or mementoes. Her office was just as impersonal. No plants. No lamps. No mirrors. No rugs on the wooden floor. Plain shelves lining the walls, laden with neatly ordered books. A set of digital clocks showing the time regions of the world. A coat rack occupied one corner, bare as a winter tree.

Mrs Magdalene wasn't interested in fancy possessions or any other displays of authority. As Vice President of Manticorps, she didn't need to show off how powerful she was.

At the other end of the room, Victor waited patiently, his huge frame making the chair he sat in look like a toy. His face was red and swollen and ugly purple bruises mottled his forehead.

"You've worked for me for quite some time." Mrs Magdalene's face was turned away, so he could only see her profile. "I've never had reason to reprimand you before."

"You still don't." Victor shifted in his seat and it creaked alarmingly. "There was no way for me to predict the situation we encountered."

"The *situation* being your four-man squad getting soundly beaten by a housewife and a couple of children."

"One child," Victor corrected. "The girl spent most of the fight under a table."

"That almost sounded sarcastic," Mrs Magdalene mused. "Surely you're not stupid enough to antagonise me. Not after yesterday's debacle."

"Simply stating the facts, Ma'am," Victor replied. "My team are all ex-servicemen and the best at what they do. Taking those people in should have been a piece of cake. It turned out to be quite the opposite."

"Enlighten me."

"The girl rumbled us and the woman started swinging a kettle about. Yeah, she got lucky and took out a couple of my men. Even so, I would have easily prevailed."

Victor shook his head, still bemused by what had happened.

"When Charlie joined in, that was something else entirely." He indicated the wounds on his head. "What he did to me wasn't luck. The kid moved like he'd had years of training in unarmed combat."

"And you had no inkling that Charlie Ray was capable of such feats? Even after watching his house for a month?"

"He never did anything out of the ordinary before. Seemed like a loser, to be honest."

"All your reports indicate that, yes." Mrs Magdalene slowly turned her head to look at him and Victor, tough as he was, repressed a shudder.

One half of the Vice President's face resembled a kindly matron. The other side was puckered and twisted, the flesh hard and bubbled as melted plastic. Her lip curled up over exposed teeth in a permanent sneer, as if her cheek had been unzipped, and one eye drooped alarmingly. The disfigurement made Victor's own injuries seem like a gnat bite.

"What do you know about Gerry Ray?" the Vice President asked.

"He's on your short list of people who might have destroyed the Marginal Science Department," Victor replied. "That's why you had us watching the house. In case he tried to contact his family."

"And the Atlas Serum?" Mrs Magdalene opened a file on her desk.

"It was supposed to enhance human capabilities in order to make super soldiers." Victor looked surprised. "I thought that had gone nowhere."

"We suffered a few setbacks but an unexpected breakthrough had the project back on track." The Vice President studied the papers in front of her. "After last night, I'd say Gerry Ray's son bears all the hallmarks of having been given just such a drug."

"He couldn't have beaten me otherwise," Victor concurred.

"I'm now utterly convinced that Gerry Ray stole our research." Mrs Magdalene stared out of the window. "Then he burned down our lab. Killed my scientists and did *this* to me."

She stroked her scars with the gloved hand again.

"Naturally, I'm very keen to find his whereabouts."

Victor stayed quiet, well aware that Mrs Magdalene wanted vengeance rather than sympathy.

"We took a couple of pictures of her in Charlie's window." Victor shook his head. "But her back was to us most of the time or it was too dark to see any features properly."

He spread large hands.

"We've no idea who she is."

"Could she just be Charlie's girlfriend?" Mrs Magdalene mulled over what she had been told. "In the wrong place at the wrong time?"

"No. In my opinion, she's more dangerous than the boy."

"What leads you to that conclusion?"

"As soon as she showed up, all our bugs went dark. Naturally, we removed them after the family fled." Victor reached into his pocket and took out a small, blackened object. "They're fried. Not turned off or disabled. Fried."

He tossed the device onto the woman's desk.

"These things are state-of-the-art. I don't know of anything that could reduce them to charred metal."

"Nostradamus could. He would also be capable of scrubbing the girl's identity from any database." Mrs Magdalene gave a thin smile, though it turned into a sinister leer on the shattered side of her face. "I assumed he was destroyed too but it looks like I was wrong. I think this girl may be the key to finding him."

She picked up the bug and studied it.

"I don't like being wrong."

"And I have no idea who Nostradamus is." Victor sounded disapproving. "I could have done my job better if I had all the facts."

Mrs Magdalene stared at him.

"Don't you *ever* criticize me." She got up and clumped round the desk. Her legs were as burned and twisted as her visage, encased in an exoskeleton of shining rods and pistons. They made a hissing noise when she walked.

Victor watched her warily.

"I want those children hunted down." The Vice President growled. "All of Manticorps' resources will be at your disposal and I'm putting you in charge of a new team. A very *special* team."

"With all due respect, Ma'am. My old squad are up to that task."

"Forget about them. They've been... retired."

Victor knew *retired* meant dead, but he showed no emotion. In his line of work, sentiments got you killed.

"Whatever secrets those brats are carrying belong to Manticorps," the woman seethed. "They're our *property.*"

She removed her glove, revealing a skeletal hand made of burnished steel. It looked like some horrible metal spider attached to her wrist.

"Yet... you let them escape."

She grabbed Victor by the throat and squeezed until his eyes bulged. The man fought for breath but didn't struggle or look away. Instead, he slid his own hand inside his jacket.

"See, *that's* why you're still in charge, Vic." Mrs Magdalene looked down at the revolver pressed against her stomach. "You don't panic easily."

She let go of his neck and grasped the gun. Spindly fingers tightened on the weapon and crumpled it like paper.

"But, if you let me down again, I'll do the same thing to your head."

- Part 2-

The Scheme

To achieve great things, two requirements are needed.

A plan and not quite enough time.

Leonard Bernstein

-14-

Leaning on the balcony rails, Charlie watched gathering clouds scudding across the sky, almost scraping the hilltops. Every now and then the sun broke through, intensifying the colour of patchwork fields.

The beauty of the landscape was lost on him. He was too busy thinking about what would happen if he failed to come up with a workable scheme. The notion made him physically ill.

"Don't get all dark and gloomy," he repeated over and over. "Remember your favourite holiday or something."

But it was hard not to succumb to fear and doubt. Despite Daffodil's reassurances, he felt utterly alone. What was Nostradamus playing at? Who could believe a mere teenager, no matter how smart, was capable of carrying out a prison break?

Charlie's eyes widened.

Who *would* believe that? Certainly no one at Sunnyside.

His mind began to jump. He sat down and wrote. *Physically ill. Who would suspect a mere child? Stick together.*

And, suddenly, he had the rest of his plan.

Charlie came back in, carrying a sheaf of notes covered in scribbled handwriting.

"You been on that balcony for two hours." Daffodil was staring at the TV, her back to him. "Writing your life story or somethin?"

"My life story wouldn't take *one* hour. And the only exciting bit would be the last couple of days." He dumped his notes on the table. "I've been thinking a lot about that. Not that I wouldn't go back to how things were."

"I had a go at a plan, myself. But I got distracted by this television set." Daffodil switched off the TV. "Didn't realise what a terrible state the world was in."

"Ah," Charlie said. "You've been watching the news."

"Nah. Something called *Britain's Got Talent*."

"You are genuinely strange." He grabbed the sheaves and handed them over. "Read this."

"You've perked up a bit."

"I've been scared to use my new-found powers but that's definitely the wrong approach in this situation." Charlie twiddled his thumbs sheepishly. "Maybe I've tried a bit *too* hard to be normal, in fact. Might have made me a bit… boring."

"You'll get no argument from me. You're as square as a dice in a box factory."

"Thanks. Thing is, whether my ability is a talent or a curse, I'll have to use it for this job. Win or lose, you won't hear any more complaints from me."

"Especially if we lose. Then everyone will be dead."

"Always look on the bright side. Now read."

Daffodil went through the pages slowly. Charlie shuffled around impatiently until she was finished.

"This is your big scheme, huh?" She put down the papers. "I got a few choice words to describe it."

"Ready and waiting."

"Insane?"

"That's one word."

"OK. It's completely and utterly insane. Also, pre-posterous, far-fetched and ludicrous." She shrugged. "Nostradamus has been teaching me more phrases."

"Oh." Charlie's face fell. "I... thought you'd like the idea."

"Have you met me?" Daffodil tweaked his nose. "I love it!"

"Stop that right now and let me talk to Nostrada-mus." The boy prised himself away. "Time to find out how good *he* is."

Some of the items you want are difficult to get hold of. The computer screen flashed up a large exclamation mark. *And by difficult, I mean damned near impossible.*

"Can't you order them on the web?" Charlie wasn't put off. "Have them secretly delivered?"

I'm pretty sure Amazon don't sell bazookas.

"Ignore that one." Daffodil chuckled. "I slipped it in for a laugh."

Fortunately, I anticipated you might need specialized equipment, so Gerry and I already made preparations. You can bask in my awesomeness later.

"It's great you're always thinking two steps ahead," Daffodil said. "But you couldn't possibly have some of the things Chaz is askin for."

Have a bit of faith. Nostradamus' lights twinkled merrily. *Meet me in the basement.*

"We have a basement?"

It's why I picked this house. There's a trapdoor in the hall cupboard.

Minutes later, the pair had descended a ladder and were standing in a vast concrete bunker running the length of the house. Wooden tables covered in vials and bottles were dotted around, along with implements and tools that the children didn't recognise. Another computer screen was fastened to the wall, blue ovals flickering across its surface.

"What is all this?"

It's the Manticorps Marginal Research Lab, or as near a recreation of it as Gerry and I could manage. In fact, it's better. Most of the projects those morons were researching hadn't even reached development stage. I got Gerry to make some modifications and now they actually work.

Nostradamus sounded smug.

He might look like the world's oldest Cockatoo nowadays, but your dad was pretty capable when it came to technology. Check this out.

The glowing dots formed an arrow on the screen, pointing to the far end of the room. On the floor was a huge white object with silver handle on the door.

"It's a fridge. Big deal."

It is a three-dimensional printer. Heard of them, Chaz? Or do you still use crayons and a blackboard?

"You use it to print actual objects, rather than just words on paper." Charlie remembered seeing a programme about it on Channel 4. "I can't get my head round that. But I know they're pretty basic."

Not the one I designed. Want a demonstration?

"Sure," Daffodil said. "I'll have a double fudge sundae with chocolate sprinkles. And a pony."

Put it on your birthday list.

"I would if I knew when my Goddamned birthday was."

All in good time. Right now I'm hacking into the Department of Motor Vehicles and The Ford Motor Company databases.

Nostradamus paused dramatically.

I send that information to the printer.

The machine began to whir.

It extracts elements from the air and combines them, layer upon layer, until it makes an exact replica of whatever you want. Cool, huh?

The box pinged and the door opened. Two yellow rectangles lay inside.

Fake number plates for the van in the garage, as you requested. I can also produce paint, so you can re-spray it and have transport. The vehicle already has tinted windows, so nobody will see there are only kids inside.

"Nice of Manticorps to give us a van filled with the latest technology and surveillance equipment," Charlie said. "That'll come in handy."

I can also hack Sunnyside's databases to give you plans of the prison, the location of each inmate and de-tails about the guards and other staff.

"Please do that. Can you give a rough overview right now?"

Natch. The screen gave a thumbs-up emoji. *The fa-cility has 200 warders and the White Spider is in the isolation block, reserved for the most dangerous crim-inals. The cells and corridors have doors with electronic locks that I can open and close but, once you leave the wing, you'd have to cross a large central compound to reach the main gate.*

"In full view of any guards outside."

Yup. Plus the gate has double reinforced steel doors. They aren't electronic, so I can't move them. And the wall is fifteen feet high with barbed wire on top.

"Can you shut down the alarms?

Most of them, but there are hand-cranked sirens in the event of a power cut. They go off and squad cars full of armed response officers will be on the scene within 10 minutes. Any inmate actually making it past them will be hunted by police helicopters and tracker dogs.

"Much as I hate to agree with Chaz," Daffodil breathed. "This *is* impossible."

"No." Charlie held up his hand. "It's pretty much as I expected. What about the last thing I asked for?"

The chemical compound? Nothing like that has ever been invented. I'd have to work out a very intricate formula from scratch.

"Oh." The boy couldn't hide his disappointment. "How long will it take?"

Might be up to an hour.

"I didn't like you at first, Nostradamus," the boy nodded approvingly. "But you're growing on me."

Like two peas in a pod, eh?

"Don't push it."

Daffodil glanced at Charlie hoping he might say something nice about her, but he was busy investigating the room. She gave a sigh and joined in.

"Hey, I found a second printer." She opened the door of another white box. "Wow! You replicated bottles of coke."

That is *a fridge.*

"Oh," she blushed. "Can I have one?"

Knock yourself out. Don't drink the stuff myself. Distinct lack of lips.

"Back to business," Charlie commanded. "Can you look like a human being, Nostradamus? On the screen, I mean."

Why? What's wrong with the way I am?

"I'd like to have an actual person to talk to."

If you insist. You and the printer aren't the only ones who can copy things. That was another pun, by the way.

The dots on the screen congealed until a face appeared. It resembled Charlie, but with Daffodil's hair and eyes.

How about this? Nostradamus smiled maniacally. There was a huge gap between his two front teeth.

"Hahahahahah!" Daffodil elbowed her horrified companion. "If we had kids, that's what they'd look like!"

"I'm not even going there." Charlie squinted through his fingers. "Can you change to something that won't give me nightmares?"

Shame. I was going for a flying octopus next.

Nostradamus morphed into Marion Ray. Though it looked similar to the real person, there was no spark of warmth in the pixilated eyes.

"Absolutely not. That's more disturbing than I can put into words."

Boy, you're hard to please.

The face altered again. It was angular, with high cheekbones, a fringe-like beard and a top hat.

"Abraham Lincoln?" Daffodil chuckled. "Are you kidding me?"

I cannot tell a lie, young lady. The voice was deep and gravelly. *I trust you will find this an acceptable visage.*

"Aw, just go back to being dots and emojis." Charlie gave up. "And give us the low-down on the White Spider."

The White Spider is a mercenary who fought for Manticorps in Iraq and Afghanistan. A map of the Middle East flashed up on the screen. *Apparently, he murdered his entire squad out there, though it was never proved. Snuck back to into Britain and couldn't adjust to civilian life. Got into a fight in some bar and killed three ex-servicemen with his bare hands. A thoroughly nasty piece of work.*

"With a friend like that, who needs enemies?" Charlie gasped. "What if he kills someone else while he's on the loose?"

He'll be a fugitive in hiding. He's not likely to stroll into Sainsbury's and start shooting the place up cause they don't have his favourite brand of Cornflakes.

"Then he'd be a cereal killer," Daffodil guffawed.

"But you're happy to set him on the people at Manticorps?" Charlie tutted. "If he hates them as much as you say, won't there be carnage?"

I'll appeal to his better nature.

"I can never tell if you're joking." The boy glared at Nostradamus' screen. "I'm not sure you can either."

Says the guy with a humour bypass. Leave the damage limitation to me. I can't give you...

"...Any more details than that. Way ahead of you." Charlie took a mask and spray gun from a rack on the wall. "Right now, I have a van to paint."

"And then?" Daffodil handed him a coke.

"We break into a warehouse on the outskirts of Edinburgh."

He took a swig.

"It'll be good practise for the real thing."

-15-

The van, now painted jet black, drove silently through the back streets of Edinburgh. In the passenger seat, Daffodil had her eyes closed, a look of intense concentration on her face.

Charlie knew she was absorbing information from Nostradamus. Books. Movies. Dates. Famous people. Political movements. He assumed she was trying to make up the knowledge that had been eradicated when the chip was implanted.

"Ask him to give you the recipe for cheese scones," he said. "I'm a fiend for cheese scones."

"I'm a partner in crime, Chaz. Not your chef."

The vehicle pulled to a stop outside a complex of large, corrugated buildings surrounded by a high wire fence. Charlie cut the engine and switched off the lights, making the vehicle nearly invisible. He reached behind his seat and hauled a tin of liquid onto his lap.

"You want Warehouse 7. *Empire Cleaning Products*." Daffodil had a hand on her neck. "Nostradamus says to look for a bunch of blue plastic tanks labelled **Promundus**. Put a splash of his special formula into each. That oughtta do it."

She lowered her voice.

"What if the place is guarded?"

"There's nothing important enough in there to need a night watchman," Charlie replied. "Except to us. Stay in the van and don't touch anything."

He got out of the vehicle and scaled the fence, container in one hand.

Daffodil watched as he crept over to the window of Warehouse 7. It was beyond his reach, so Charlie balanced several discarded wooden crates underneath and clambered up. There was a soft tinkle of breaking glass and he vanished inside.

"*Stay in the van and don't touch anything.*" She mimicked her partner's voice. "When are you gonna stop treating me like some kinda lackey?"

She unwrapped the sandwiches she had brought for the wait and took a bite.

"Seemsh like you and Nostradamus don't hardly need me anymore." Daffodil chewed angrily. "Well, I'm jusht as valuable a part of this team ash you two."

She leaned on the steering wheel and the horn beeped loudly.

"No, no!" Daffodil dropped the sandwich in horror and it landed on the dirty floor.

"Guess I really am useless. Can't do nothin right."

She looked out of the window to see if anyone had been alerted by the noise.

"What the…?"

Three ominous shapes flitted along the side of the buildings, low to the ground. They stopped under the window that was Charlie's way in and out.

"Dobermans!" Daffodil winced. "We are officially knee-deep in doggie do-do."

The hounds lay down behind the pile of wooden crates and waited for Charlie to emerge again.

"No wonder this place don't need a night watchman." Daffodil jumped out of the van. "Chaz aint gonna see those mutts til it's too late."

She grabbed her sandwiches, ran to the fence and quickly climbed to the top. The Dobermans spotted her and loped towards the new intruder.

Daffodil threw the bread slices as hard as she could. They landed several yards away and the dogs rushed over to devour them. The window creaked open and Charlie began to wriggle through the gap.

"Guard dogs!" she hissed. "Stay where you are, Chaz, or your butt's gonna get munched!"

"What'll I do?" He shot her a look of panic.

"Nothin as stupid as this, I hope." Daffodil leapt from the top of the fence and landed in the enclosure with a grunt. Then she was on her feet and running towards Charlie. The dogs abandoned the sandwiches and raced after her.

She scrambled up the crates with the animals snapping at her heels.

"You're the muscle, Chaz," she gasped, as Charlie pulled her to safety. "Can you take em?"

"Not three monsters that size," he gulped. "Besides, I'm... eh... scared of dogs. It's more of a phobia, really."

"Oh, that's *fantastic*. I been sitting thinkin you're tougher than a hobnail boot in a pickle jar and you suddenly have a weak spot."

"The van's filled with surveillance equipment," Charlie said hopefully. "Can Nostradamus transmit a high frequency signal that will hurt those dogs' ears enough to drive them away?"

"He says animals don't hear radio waves." Daffodil shook her head. "A really loud bang will scare them, but it'll also attract attention."

"We can't just sit here!" Charlie looked anxiously at the canines. "Every minute we hang around increases our chances of being discovered."

Daffodil tapped her neck and listened.

"Well, I guess I'm the expendable one." She grabbed the tin, took a deep breath and jumped.

"Mac!" Charlie shouted. "What are you doing?"

Daffodil landed on one hound and smacked another across its snout with the metal can. The surprised creatures bounded away but stopped after a few yards. Then they turned and advanced, bellies scraping the ground and lips pulled back over drooling fangs. Daffodil knelt and started scooping stones into the can, never taking her eyes off the dogs. They began to make little runs at her before retreating again.

"Chaz? When they attack, run for the fence."

Charlie hesitated. But, no matter how scared he was, he couldn't let Daffodil face the creatures alone.

"The hell I will." He landed beside her, sending up a puff of dirt. "Ladies first."

"How very old-fashioned." The girl stood up. "But, according to Nostradamus, sometimes old-fashioned works."

She began to shake the tin. The stones bounced around inside, making a hollow booming noise. The Dobermans began to back away, whining and pawing the dirt.

"Sounds like thunder, don't it?" Daffodil moved forwards, still rattling the tin. "An pooches are terrified of thunder."

She hurled the canister and the beasts took off again, genuinely frightened this time.

"Go!" She sprinted for the fence, her partner close behind. They reached the top as the creatures came racing back, leaping and snarling but unable to reach their quarry.

"Nice work, Mac." Charlie helped her over and down. "I owe you one."

"Can you go back for my sandwiches then? I'm starving."

"Very funny. We'll order pizza when we get home."

-16-

"That was a neat trick back there." Charlie hunched over the wheel on the drive back to Dalmahoy. "Quick thinking too."

"I ain't just a pretty face, Chaz." Daffodil batted her eyelids.

"Don't believe I mentioned your looks."

"You're a master at shutting people out, know that?"

"Why didn't Nostradamus warn us about the dogs?" Charlie shifted gears as smoothly as the subject.

"He doesn't want too many details, remember? So you didn't tell him exactly what we were gonna do." She scratched her cheek. "It just proves we can't always depend on him to fix things. We really are on our own."

They drove in silence for a while.

"You risked your life for me," Charlie said eventually. "After I've been so rotten to you."

"That mean you're gonna be nice from now on?"

"Nah. You're still a royal pain."

"Don't matter." Daffodil grinned. "You risked your life for me too."

"Can't allow you to die just yet. You're part of my cunning plan."

"In other words, we're a team."

"All right," Charlie sighed. "We're a team."

Daffodil's smile widened.

"We should have a name. Like the Dynamic Duo." She tapped her fingers together. "I know. The Army of Two!"

"That's an X-Box Game."

"Still not sure what an X-Box is but I'll take your word for it." The girl thought hard. "How about the Armageddon Twins?"

"That *is* catchy," Charlie conceded. "As long as people don't think we're actually related."

"The Armageddon Twins." Daffodil took up a fighting stance. "Saving the world, one mistake at a time." She punched out at an invisible enemy. "Pow! Pow!"

"Don't make me regret agreeing to this."

"We should have capes. And masks," she giggled. "I got a pair of tights you can wear."

"Please stop."

"We can have business cards printed."

"If I can get a word in, I was going apologise." Charlie pulled into the driveway of their house. "I never really thought about how it must feel. Not remembering who you are."

"Pretty crappy. But I reckon little bits are starting to come back."

"Really? Like what?"

"I think I used to live in a big house," Daffodil said. "A mansion, in fact. I reckon I might have been pretty well off."

"Anything else?"

"It had a library. All polished wood and leather couches. I used to spend hours reading anything I could get my hands on. Old detective and western novels were my favourites."

She thought hard.

"It's all pretty hazy and I can't recall anything else." She shrugged. "Anyhow, Nostradamus promised to tell me everything when this is over, so I guess I'll just have to wait."

"He seems to have warmed to us but I still don't trust him." Charlie switched off the ignition. "I'm going to do a little digging of my own, when I get the chance."

"That ain't got much to go on."

"No. But I can't see a good reason why he'd keep your past secret. Not now that you're committed to helping." He looked at her quizzically. "Unless there's something terrible lurking there."

"Very tactful." Daffodil sighed. "You sure know how to sweet-talk a girl."

"I got oodles of charm, don't I?"

"Actually, you can be quite charismatic when it suits you."

"Nostradamus teaching you big words again?"

"Chaz?" Daffodil laid a hand on his arm. "I gotta ask. How come I never seen you laugh? Or even smile?"

Charlie glanced round at her and, for a second, it looked like he might answer. Then the moment passed.

"C'mon, Mac." He jumped out and opened the passenger door.

"Let's get that pizza."

So you made it back in one piece? Nostradamus swirled around the computer screen as a series of triangles.

"We did good, Nostradamus." Daffodil mumbled through a mouthful of pizza. "What's next?"

Ask Charlie. He's the boss in this caper.

Charlie was already leafing through sheets of information on Sunnyside's staff and inmates that Nostradamus had printed out. He picked out a picture of a young, red-headed woman.

"Sammy McLaren. A nurse in the prison infirmary." He helped himself to a slice. "She's perfect."

This woman? What's so special about her?

"Because, according to your data, she's in trouble. We can use her and help her at the same time."

"You're *enjoying* this!" Daffodil studied her partner. He was still crabby and abrasive but seemed to have thawed slightly. She wondered if it was the drug or simply the awakening of an adventurous spirit which had been hidden under layers of self-doubt.

Charlie rifled through more pages and selected a mug shot. It was a handsome man holding up a card with his prison number stencilled on it.

"And this guy. Scotty Primo. Another inmate at Sunnyside."

"He's a grifter," Daffodil said. "A con man."

How did you know? Nostradamus inquired.

"No scars on his face or knuckles, so he's not into violence. His hands ain't got calluses, which means his crimes don't involve anything physical. Dude's hair is neatly combed and he's posing worse than a male model, even in a mug shot. He's careful about his appearance." She picked up Primo's folder. "This is a guy who uses looks and charisma to get what he wants."

That was pretty astute. I'm impressed.

"I'm understudying for Chaz in case he gets eaten by dogs."

"Very funny."

"Primo's doing ten years," Daffodil whistled. "That's a pretty big sentence for a scam artist."

"It's because he conned some very rich people out of a lot of money and won't say where it's stashed." Charlie pinned the pictures to the basement wall. "We need the help of both these people if this is going to work."

"What if they won't play ball?"

"They will if we push the right buttons."

I can't allow you to harm anyone, Nostradamus warned. *Told you already.*

"I've no intention of hurting them. Quite the opposite." Charlie wiped a sliver of cheese from his chin. "Nostradamus, I'll need cash. A lot of cash."

I can hack any bank account undetected. Already donated a few Russian oligarchs' life savings to Amnesty International, as a matter of fact.

"I got some new villains lined up to steal money from." Charlie began to tidy away the empty pizza boxes. "Then I'll deal with Sammy McLaren. Daffodil?"

"Yup?"

"You're going to have a little chat with Mr Primo. Nostradamus will tell you what to say."

"I ain't a glove puppet, Chaz." She pinged an olive at him. "I'm quite capable of doin my own talking. In fact, I never shut up."

"Yeah," Charlie said. "I had noticed."

Daffodil presented her fake ID to the reception desk of Sunnyside Prison.

"This is very unusual." The receptionist looked disconcerted. "Unaccompanied children aren't normally permitted to make visits."

"My mum and I are only in the country a short while and she isn't well." Daffodil handed over a permission slip. "So the Home Office made an exception."

"That's an interesting accent. American?"

"I'm from South Africa."

"Oh. Well, these look to be in order." The woman studied the perfectly forged papers that Nostradamus had printed. "You'll have to be searched for contraband, even if you are a minor."

"That's all right." Daffodil allowed herself to be frisked, then walked through the scanner. She half expected her chip to set off the alarm but Nostradamus was encased in plastic and remained invisible to the detection devices. Her picture was taken and she was given a visitor pass to clip on her lapel.

"All done." The warder on duty waved her through.

This security system sucks. Nostradamus muttered in her head. *They deserve to lose a prisoner or two. Maybe persuade them to try a bit harder in the future.*

Scotty Primo was led to a small plastic table in the communal room of Sunnyside Prison.

"You don't get visitors very often." The guard sat him down. "And you never mentioned having a daughter before."

"First time she's ever set foot in the place, boss." Scotty said dolefully. "I haven't seen her in years."

"Tough break." The man shrugged and walked off. Everyone in here had a hard-luck story and he'd heard them all before.

The door opened with a buzz and Daffodil edged in. Spotting Scotty, she rushed across the room and squeezed him tightly.

"Hello dad!"

"Hi, honey. Take a seat." Scotty glanced round to make sure the guard wasn't listening, but the man was already engrossed in conversation with one of his workmates.

"I'm an inquisitive type," Scotty said softly. "Which is why I agreed to this request for a visit. Problem is, I don't *have* a daughter."

Daffodil studied the man. He was in his late thirties and even more handsome in real life than the mug shot. He was well-spoken and his piercing green eyes rarely blinked.

"Yes, you do," she said. "But your ex-wife won't let her communicate with you. Can't imagine why."

She snapped her fingers.

"Oh. Maybe cause you're a convicted criminal and probably not the best role model a young girl could have."

"OK. You've done your homework." The man nodded. "And you must have some pretty convincing documents, or you wouldn't have made it through that door by impersonating her."

He gave a smile and his eyes twinkled. It made him look both likeable and trustworthy.

"I certainly appreciate the company." The smile widened. "But I still want to know why you're pretending to be my kid."

"Dial down the sexyometer, bub. I ain't the swooning type." Daffodil kept her voice low. "My accomplices and I are going to break you out. In return for a favour."

"I've only got five years left of my sentence to serve," Scotty replied calmly. "I don't want to be broken out, even if it were possible."

"It's possible."

"No thanks." Primo turned to beckon the guard.

"I understand your reluctance. You *had* £2,000,000 you conned outta fat cats stashed in a bank account in the Cayman Islands. Only it's gone."

"Say that again." The smile vanished.

"Sort code 45 85 96. Account number 1887 2256 3148." Daffodil reeled off the numbers Nostradamus was relaying to her. "We emptied it."

Scotty's mouth opened but no sound came out.

"That enough of an incentive for ya, buddy?"

"The money I hid was to set my daughter up in life," Primo replied acidly. "My *real* daughter."

"Then she's gonna be a damned sight poorer."

Scotty Primo was a practical man. This girl had his bank details and how she got them wasn't important right now. She was obviously a force to be reckoned with.

"You have my attention."

Daffodil slipped a hand inside her shirt, clicked open a catch on her pendant, and removed three tiny pills.

"These oughtta be small enough to hide on your person." She took Scotty's hand and slid the capsules into his palm. "You take one and you convince a convict called the White Spider to take the other. They'll give you a temperature an bring you out in a rash, but there won't be no long-term effects. However, it'll land you both in the prison infirmary and we'll be able to break you out from there."

"Then the answer's *definitely* no."

"No?" Daffodil was taken aback.

"I conned rich people. Nasty rich people." The man glared at her. "But I've never killed anyone. I'm certainly not helping put a sadistic animal like the White Spider back on the streets."

"I take it you don't like the guy."

"This place contains some of the most hardened criminals in the country," Scotty replied. "Men who have slaughtered women and children without blinking an eye. Guys who aren't afraid of anything."

He shuddered.

"Except the White Spider. He's sinister beyond words. He scares the *guards*, for God's sakes."

"He'll only be free for a short time. Then we'll turn him over to the police."

"You expect me to believe that?" Scotty laughed out loud and the prison officer looked around.

"Just sharing a father, daughter joke, boss!" he called.

"Nice to see you're getting along." The warder checked his watch. "You got ten minutes left."

"Fine." Daffodil said nonchalantly. "There are a dozen inmates in here we can use instead."

"Then do so. This conversation is over."

"All right. We'll put the money back into your account."

"You'll do what?" It was Scotty's turn to look flabbergasted.

"If you intended to keep your ill-gotten gains, we'd take the lot. But your daughter ain't a criminal, so it's not fair to deprive her of a decent life." Daffodil got up to leave. "Good to know you got *some* morals."

"Sit down." Scotty stared into her eyes. "I'm the best con man in the business and I always know when someone's playing me."

He sat back and rubbed his head.

"You're telling the *truth*."

"Here's something else to think about." Daffodil held his stare. "Your daughter don't need money. She needs a dad in her life."

"Yeah? What good is a father who's always looking over his shoulder, in case the law closes in?"

"We'll provide you with a new identity and tell you where your daughter is, if you wanna risk seeing her," Daffodil said. "I sure hope you try."

"You don't know where *your* parents are, kid." Scotty tightened his grip. "Do you?"

"You're certainly good at reading people." The girl smiled sadly. "I don't even know *who* they are, but I'd give anything to find out."

"A great liar can always spot when someone is being insincere." The man ran a hand down his face. "And you're not."

"We're the good guys, Mr Primo. Honest injun."

"Who is the third pill for?"

"The prison doctor. Slip it into his drink when you get to the infirmary." Daffodil reddened slightly. "I hate to have an innocent man suffer but, like I say, it won't have no long-term effects. He'll be right as rain in a couple of days."

"I need to think about it."

"It's a one-time offer." She snapped her locket shut. "Turn me down and you'll have five long years to ponder your missed opportunity."

"You can really pull this off?"

"It should have been impossible for me to get this far. But here I am."

"I want to see my daughter more than you could imagine." Scotty pocketed the pills. "So count me in. But if this prison break goes wrong, I'll find a way to convince the authorities I was a victim and not an accomplice."

"I'm sure you will. You're slippier than a weasel coated in axle grease."

"Also, are you positive the White Spider *wants* out of jail?"

"Why wouldn't he? He's got a life sentence."

"Because he's as crazy as a loon, by all accounts. He actually seems to like it here."

Daffodil took on a faraway look, as if she were listening to some voice Scotty couldn't hear.

"Time's up, kid," the guard shouted.

"If he won't co-operate, tell him this." She leaned forward, kissed the man on the cheek and whispered a sentence in his ear.

"I don't even know what that *means*," Scotty said dubiously.

"It'll work. My source is never wrong."

Daffodil got up and left with the guard, leaving the grifter to consider just what he had agreed to.

Daffodil climbed into the van parked outside the prison gates.

"Primo's on board," she announced. "We can't take his money, neither. It's for his daughter."

"Are you sure he didn't con you about that?" Charlie was sitting behind the wheel. "It's what he does."

"Not at all," Daffodil replied. "But I gave my word and I aint about to break it."

"That's all right. We have another bank account to empty. And this one belongs to a proper scumbag."

Charlie started the engine and drove off.

"My turn now. Tomorrow we're going to rescue prison nurse Sammy McLaren from an extremely bad situation."

You might want to consider something. Nostradamus spoke from one of the monitors in the back of the vehicle. *Nobody knows who Daffodil is, but I made the security cameras a bit blurry, just in case. Her prints and ID will also vanish from Sunnyside's systems when this is over. You're a different kettle of fish, Charlie.*

"In what way?"

The shootout at your house has been on the news, along with your picture. I can wipe the CCTV near Miss McLaren's house, but a passer-by might still recognize you. You better wear a disguise.

"As long as it's nothing like my dad's effort," Charlie said. "Besides, I'm too young to grow a moustache."

"Ooh! Ooh! I know!" Daffodil held up her hand. "I got the perfect camouflage."

This is bound to be good. What have you got in mind?

She told them both her idea.

"I am *not* doing that," Charlie fumed. "No way. Not a chance."

You're turning out to be quite an asset, Mac. Nostradamus laughed. *I'd pay serious money to see this.*

"Not doing it." The boy repeated.

I'll replicate the things we need. Sorry, Chaz.

"Daffodil?" Charlie glowered.

"I really hate you right now."

-18-

Sammy McLaren sat on the couch, arm around her young son. The doorbell rang and they both flinched.

"Hide in your room, honey." She patted the boy's head. "It'll be all right. I promise."

The child held on tight, refusing to let go.

"Please, Gus. I'll be fine."

Her son plodded tearfully through to his bedroom. Sammy went to the door and slowly opened it.

Charlie stood on the step. His face was painted white and he sported a red rubber nose and painted-on grin, topped by a huge orange wig. He wore a spotted clown suit, frilly collar and giant flappy shoes. In one hand he held a large tartan bag. In the other, he clutched the strings of a bunch of balloons, which floated above his head like a multicoloured cloud.

"Miss McLaren?" he said. "You've won two free tickets to the circus. May I come in?"

"You have to go away, son. I don't want free tickets." Sammy looked nervously up and down the street. "I'm… I'm expecting visitors."

"Yes. You're waiting for Ryan Cardownie. He's a loan shark and you owe him several thousand pounds. Only you don't have the cash to pay him back."

"Oh." Sammy instantly turned hostile. "You work for him, you little monster."

"If I did, I wouldn't have turned up looking like I escaped from crazy town." Charlie stuck his giant foot in the door before Sammy could shut it. "I'm actually here to pay off your debt."

He opened the bag. It was stuffed to the brim with £100 notes.

"Now, can I come in?"

"Why would you help me?" Sammy sat on a chair opposite the boy. "And how come you're dressed like that?"

"No time for discussion. Mr Cardownie is always prompt." Charlie looked at a big yellow watch decorated with ladybirds. "He'll be here any second."

"And then?"

"I'll make him go away." He curled up in his own chair trying to get his feet to behave. The balloons bobbed and swayed above him, bumping into the walls and ceiling. "You get into the bedroom with your son and I'll handle it."

"Handle it?" Sammy couldn't believe her ears. "How old are you? Thirteen?"

"I'm fifteen. And I'm not alone."

"Ryan Cardownie is a vicious thug and he'll have his gang with him." Sammy was close to tears. "There's much more in that bag than the amount I owe. He'll take it all."

"He'll certainly try." Charlie waved her away. "You go and look after Gus. I imagine he's freaking out."

"I'm not leaving you with that guy. You're a child!"

"Let's just say I have a rather unique set of skills."

"What? Making balloon animals?" She glared at him. "Wait. Is this some kind of police sting, with you as the decoy?"

"That's absolutely right," Charlie lied.

"I don't see any unmarked vehicles parked here." Sammy peeked round the curtains. "Just the usual cars."

"If you could spot a sting, so could Ryan," the boy pointed out. "We have a surveillance van in the next street and I'm wearing a wire."

The doorbell rang.

"It's him!" Sammy looked round in terror. "Oh, God."

"Off you go," Charlie repeated. "Don't come out until I tell you, no matter what kind of commotion you hear."

"Thank you, whoever you are." Sammy vanished into the bedroom.

The bell rang again, but Charlie ignored it. A few seconds later there was a crash as the front door was kicked open.

Two men strode into the living room, led by Ryan Cardownie. He was well built, with slicked-down hair, a spotty face and an arrogant stance.

"Evening gentlemen." Charlie raised a white-gloved hand in greeting. "I take it you've come about an unpaid debt?"

"Who the hell are you, Coco?" Ryan narrowed his eyes. "Why are you dressed like some freak?"

"I like to spread joy and happiness," the boy gurned. "Got a problem with that?"

"I'll be happy when I get my cash. Where is it?"

"Miss McLaren owes you four grand." He pointed to the open bag on the table. "Take that amount and bugger off."

Ryan pulled the valise towards him.

"There's a fortune in here!" he smirked nastily. "Unfortunately, my interest rate has suddenly just gone up, so I'll be having all of it."

He rifled through the contents and gave a sharp intake of breath.

"There are thousands in here!"

"Six hundred thousand and forty pounds, to be accurate." Charlie corrected. "I'm sure you recognise the figure. It's the exact amount that *used* to be in your private account."

"This is *my* money?" Ryan went purple. "How...?"

"No matter what bank you use, we'll hack it." Charlie yawned. "Which means you're going to find it hard to pay your accomplices."

The henchman glanced at each other.

"Not now I've got it back, moron." Ryan motioned to his companions. "Let's do some serious damage to this midget."

"You don't want to take that route." The boy held up a large pin. "It'll make me a very angry clown. And I'm not in the best of moods on *any* day."

"You're going to fight us with a needle?" Ryan closed in on him, his heavies right behind. "Now *that's* funny."

Charlie took a deep breath and held it, then reached up and popped a large red balloon. A puff of incandescent dust enveloped the loan shark and he reeled away, gagging and clawing at his throat.

The boy was on his gigantic feet in a second. A jet of acidic liquid squirted from a plastic daisy on his lapel and hit the first yob in the face. The man clutched at his eyes as Charlie jabbed the pin into his leg and twisted. The thug sank to his knees and shuffled away, groaning in pain. The second assailant swung at his diminutive adversary, but he ducked, pulled a rubber chicken from his voluminous pocket and smacked the man across the head. The thug flew backwards, smashing through the glass coffee table, unconscious before he landed.

"Got an iron bar inside," Charlie explained, knocking out the second yob as he tried to crawl to safety. "Your turn now Ryan."

"Get away from me!" The loan shark ran round the broken table, coughing and gasping, with Charlie waddling in pursuit, his enormous feet flapping on the carpet. He leapt into the air and landed on the thug's back, arms around his neck.

He tightened his grip and held on until Ryan collapsed and passed out.

"This is so undignified. I should have run away and joined the library instead."

He took a pair of plastic garden ties from his other pocket and fastened the man's hands behind his back. Then he grabbed a vase from the window sill and poured water over him.

"I will kill you for this!" The loan shark sat up, spluttering and shaking his head. "You'll *never* be safe."

"You don't even know what I look like under this makeup." Charlie pushed the brute down and sat on him. "Thing is, that smart TV in the corner has a video cam, which my accomplice controls. Tomorrow I'm going to post our little fight on YouTube, along with your name and address."

"You wouldn't dare!" Ryan tried to buck him off.

"Nobody will spot the toxic gas I used on you," Charlie said. "It's almost invisible. What they'll see is Ryan Cardownie and his mates roughed up by a child in a clown suit. You'll never be able to intimidate anyone again."

He leaned closer.

"If that's not enough, we also recorded you telling your goons to beat up a kid. That'll land you quite a stretch in prison. And you can't afford a good lawyer anymore."

"What do you want?" Ryan stopped struggling.

"I want you to leave this family alone, get out of town, and never come back." Charlie held his pin to the man's throat. "Because, if you do, my associates will be waiting. And *they* don't clown around."

"Look, we can work out a deal…"

"In your dreams." He whacked Ryan over the head with the chicken. "Goodnight."

"You seem to have everything sewn up." Daffodil strolled in and fastened a strip of tape over Ryan's mouth. "I'll hog tie the other two, though it don't look like they'll wake any time soon. When they do, it'll take them a few hours to get free."

"Thanks, Mac."

Charlie picked up the bag and clumped into the bedroom. Sammy McLaren was on the bed with her son. The boy was sobbing into her shoulder.

"You won't be bothered by these louts again." He dropped the tartan holdall. "In this bag is £600,000 and some loose change. Take it and go start a new life. Right now."

"You're not with the police, are you?" Sammy's eyes were red-rimmed.

"Does it matter?"

"And you don't want anything in return? For all that money?"

"Send me a postcard. I hear the south of France is a nice place to live."

"I only got in debt because I wanted a few decent things for my boy." Sammy got up and squeezed her son tightly. "I don't make much on a hospital salary."

"No need to explain."

"C'mon, Gus." The woman pulled the boy to his feet. "Let's get out of this terrible place."

"Thank you, Mr Clown." The child said. "For helping my mum."

"Seems I'm in the saving business, whether I want to be or not." Charlie patted his head. "Pack anything important to you but make it quick. You have enough cash to buy whatever else you need."

"This is my mobile number." Sammy handed him a card. "If you ever need anything, just call."

"Much obliged." The boy tucked it into a spotty pocket.

He waited until Sammy McLaren had left. Then he went back to the living room, sat on Ryan again, and dialled the Sunnyside prison switchboard.

"This is Sammy McLaren," he said, imitating the woman's voice perfectly. "I need Warden Bishop to call me at home immediately. It's an emergency."

He hung up and waited. After a few minutes, the phone rang and he picked it up again.

"This is Warden Bishop. What's up Sammy?"

"You use a product called Promundus in the prison soap dispensers." Charlie continued to impersonate the nurse.

"I believe so. Why?"

"Because I work in the infirmary, I use it more than anyone else." He coughed for effect. "For the first time, it's given me a really nasty rash. I think it might be a bad batch."

"Are you all right?"

"I'll live. But, to be on the safe side, can you dump what you have and order a new supply immediately? I'd do it myself, only it looks like I'm going to be bed bound for a few days.

"That'll be expensive."

"It'll be a lot more expensive if all your guards start calling in sick."

"True." The warden sounded suitably concerned. "I'll get it done right away. Thank you for alerting me and get well soon."

"I appreciate your concern." Charlie set the receiver down.

Daffodil was watching him from the doorway.

"Well?"

"Next phase is complete. Now we have to repaint the van."

He waved her away.

"In two days, we break the Spider out of jail."

-19-

The White Spider sat on his own in Sunnyside exercise yard, reading a book, perched on a bench, his back to the wire fence. He was a tall, sinewy man with a shaved head, bug eyes and thin, cruel lips.

Nobody came near or tried to engage him in conversation, for his temper was as legendary as his ability to fight. A year ago, a convict called Carl Wicks had tried to make a reputation for himself by ambushing the Spider, backed by three of Sunnyside's most vicious hard men. All were carrying homemade weapons.

He was now known as One-Eyed Wicks and his accomplices hadn't fared much better.

Scotty shuddered at the thought of getting close to this lunatic but he had no choice. He straightened his shoulders and walked over, trying to act cool and collected.

The White Spider glanced up as Primo approached and sat down next to him.

"I have no wish to be disturbed, my good man." His tone was crisp and concise. "I intend to finish this volume by lunchtime."

"And I've no desire to disturb you." Scotty flashed his most disarming smile. "It's just that I have a proposition."

"I shall not warn you again." The White Spider returned to his paperback. "Your very presence is irritating me."

Scotty was an expert at quickly sizing people up. This maniac required a short, direct approach.

"I recently received a visit from a fifteen-year-old girl," he said. "She offered to break you and me out of prison in the next few days. Nobody else. Just us."

"That does sound intriguing," the Spider conceded. "Though I'm surprised a seasoned con artist like yourself would believe such a far-fetched notion. Especially one put to you by a mere child."

"She was extremely persuasive and I'm certain she has some serious backing." Scotty wasn't surprised that the Spider knew who he was. The creep seemed to be aware of everything that went on in Sunnyside.

"As you pointed out," he continued. "I'm a con man and not the type to fall for a scam."

"Did this girl tell you her plan?" The Spider shut his book, interest piqued.

"She didn't have the opportunity to say much, but she gave me these." Scotty opened his palm to reveal two pills. "If we take them, it'll make us appear sick enough to be moved to the infirmary. Her accomplices can break us out from there."

He felt a sharp pain in his leg and looked down.

The Spider was pressing a six-inch nail against his knee.

"The last time someone persuaded me to take a strange pill, it landed me in *this* establishment," he rasped. "So… You have until the count of three to provide me with actual information. Or you will walk with a limp for the rest of your exceedingly short life."

"That's all I know!" Scotty spluttered, sweat beading his forehead. "I'm just passing on what she said."

"One."

"Okay! She also gave me a message that I was to repeat to you."

"Two."

"She said she needed your help taking on Manticorps. Only I don't know who Manticorps are. Honestly!"

"Did she now?" The nail vanished up the Spider's sleeve as quickly as it had appeared. "Those were the exact words she uttered?"

"Wasn't hard to memorise."

"Hmmmmmm." He opened the book again, suddenly a model of politeness. "Have you read this? It's called *Grounding For The Metaphysics of Morals* by the German philosopher, Immanuel Kant. Quite fascinating."

"No," Scotty replied apprehensively. "I mostly like detective novels."

"I prefer westerns myself. But If I may quote from Kant." The Spider closed his eyes and recited. "One who makes himself a worm cannot complain after-wards if people step on him."

"Eh…. OK."

The Spider took the pill, put it between the pages and snapped the volume shut.

"I shall make my intentions plainer," he said pleas-antly. "I graciously accept your offer to remove myself from Sunnyside. If you are fooling me, however, I will grind you under the heel of my boot until you are dust."

He stood up.

"I look forward to seeing you in the infirmary. Try not to be tardy. I am not known for my patience."

He left without a backwards glance, leaving Scotty sitting rigid with fear.

Victor entered the briefing room, accompanied by Mrs Magdalene. Two men and a woman sat round the table.

"This is your new team," the Vice President said. "I'll let them introduce themselves."

"Markus Gantz." A young man with a crew cut, glasses and a T-Shirt with **FREE HUGS** written on it, stood up and extended his hand. "I am pleased to meet you."

"I'm not." Victor didn't move. "Just tell me what you do."

"I am a hacker. Nobody knows computer systems better than me."

"Nostradamus does." Victor countered. "I've now read the files and, apparently, part of him *is* a computer."

"You seem a very negative guy." Markus sat back down. "I do not think we will be friends."

"No free hug, then? My heart bleeds."

Victor nodded to the woman. She was young and extremely pretty, with an innocent face and wide blue eyes.

"What about you, blondie? In charge of makeup?"

"Candy-Anne." She studied her pointed nails. "I… retire people."

"That so?" Victor tensed.

"Yes. Make another sexist comment and I'll demonstrate."

Victor turned to the last member. He was almost as large as the leader, with long, jet-black hair tucked under a baseball cap. Round his hand was a length of chain.

"You are?"

"Hill Rylander," he replied laconically. "I'm a tracker. Old school. If Markus can identify a rough location where the kids are holed up, I'll do the rest."

"How?" Victor was unimpressed. "You going to sniff the ground? Follow a trail of broken leaves?"

"Sort of." Hill pulled on the chain and a large white shape emerged from under the table. "Meet Willie."

The hairs stood up on their leader's neck. The dog was huge. White and hairless, with malevolent pink eyes and jaws that looked like they could take a chunk out of solid metal. It glared at him and gave a throaty growl.

"Jeez." He quickly regained his composure. "Bit of an ugly brute."

"You don't want to antagonise Willie." Hill covered the dog's pointy ears. "He's very sensitive."

"I was talking about you."

"Willie was a normal looking pooch at one time," Mrs Magdalene said. "Until we tested our version of the Atlas Serum on it."

"I can see why you're so keen to have the perfected formula back." Victor regarded the mutant hound with distaste. "The old batch has a few nasty side effects."

"It does." The woman accepted. "But now Willie has a nose that can pick out an individual in a crowded football stadium."

"Find a rough location of where the fugitives might be and let him get the scent." Hill patted the slavering beast. "He'll track them to the ends of the earth."

"As long as you three follow him, I'll be satisfied."

"I thought we were chasing kids, Mrs M," Candy-Anne said softly. "Not being led by one."

"Victor was quite attached to his old squad," the Vice President explained. "But his bark is worse than his bite."

"Quite the opposite of Willie, then," Hill remarked. "I know which one I prefer."

"I'll leave you to it." Mrs Magdalene turned to go. "Stop moping and play nice, Victor."

"That dog will tear the children apart if it catches them." The giant stopped her. "I thought you wanted Charlie Ray taken alive."

"Charlie's blood is all we need to extract the perfected serum," Mrs Magdalene corrected. "And I presume the girl, given what she's capable of, is carrying Nostradamus on some kind of chip or external hard drive. Perhaps in a laptop. I simply want it retrieved."

"Yes. It is Nostradamus we really want to get hold of." Markus took off his glasses and wiped them. "If this artificial intelligence is as good as you claim, it will be able to replicate all Manticorps' lost research. I will extract that information from him. Never fear."

"So we don't need the kids." The Vice President shrugged. "If they resist, you can kill them."

"I was hoping you'd say that," Candy-Anne giggled impishly.

"Or else I'd have nothing fun to do."

-Part 3-

"I keep my valuable things locked up. Everyone does. Therefore, prisoners must be valuable."

Jarod Kintz

-20-

Daffodil was led into the waiting room of Sunny-side Prison, carrying a bunch of flowers. Once again, she handed the receptionist her fake ID and permission slips.

"I'm here to visit my dad," she said. "Scotty Primo."

"You didn't get our phone message?" The woman behind the desk looked distressed. "He's in the prison infirmary."

"The infirmary?" Daffodil feigned surprise. "Is he all right?"

"He has a temperature and a rash," the receptionist said. "So, I'm afraid you can't see him. Visits can only be conducted in the communal area."

"But I'm going back to Africa with my mum tomor-row. She works in a hospital there. It's my last chance."

"Those are the rules, I'm afraid."

"I brought him roses." Daffodil's lip quivered.

"I'm really sorry."

The girl burst into tears.

"I came all the way from Aberdeen by myself," she sobbed. "On the train. If I go back now, there's nobody coming to meet me for hours."

"There's nothing I can do, petal," the woman replied wretchedly. "It's protocol."

"I wanted to say goodbye," Daffodil wailed, laying it on as thick as she dared. "I never told him I loved him and now he's sick."

Two guards turned from their conversation and walked over.

"It's all right, Muriel." The older warder laid a hand on her arm. "Once the girl's been scanned and searched, I'll get Jake here to escort her."

His companion nodded assent.

"Primo's a model prisoner and this kid can't be more than fifteen. It's not like she has a crowbar in those flowers."

He patted Daffodil's head.

"Though you *will* have to leave the bouquet behind. Just in case."

"The White Spider is in the infirmary too, sir." Muriel hissed. "He's *not* a model prisoner."

"The Spider is in another room under heavy restraint," the senior guard replied calmly. "I can authorise it if you call the warden and let him know. He's got a daughter about the same age. He'll be sympathetic."

"On you go then, love." Muriel stamped Daffodil's papers. "I suppose I'm being a worry wart."

"C'mon, kid." The junior guard beckoned to her. "Let's get you to your father. Where's that accent from, anyhow? Spain?"

Daffodil sighed.

They walked down the corridors together, the girl making a mental note of where everything was. While Jake's back was turned, she held her breath until her face was red.

"You alright?" He glanced around. "You're all sweating and flushed."

"Don't feel too good," Daffodil slowly exhaled, throwing in a dramatic shiver for effect. "I hope I didn't make my dad ill. I visited him a couple of days ago."

"I'm sure it'll be fine." All the same, the guard quickened his step, putting a few feet between himself and his escort.

"Just don't sneeze on me. I got holidays coming up."

The phone rang in Warden Bishop's office.

"Yes?"

"It's the Health Protection Agency in Collindale." His secretary sounded alarmed. "They need to speak to you urgently."

"Put them through."

In the van, parked three miles away, Charlie was ready and waiting, mobile in hand.

"This is Douglas Livingstone from the HPA," he said in a deep baritone voice that he'd copied from the star of a medical drama on TV. "You have a nurse working for you called Sammy McLaren?"

"We do," the Warden replied. "She's off sick."

"Then I'll make this brief. We've just been at her house and suspect she has a virulent form of the James River Fever. It's highly contagious and we can't work out how she got it. It's usually confined to remote regions of central Africa."

"There was a girl called Audrey Primo here a couple of days ago, visiting her father." The warden paled. "Her papers said she'd recently been in Africa, where her mum works in a…. hospital."

"Oh, dear," Charlie said. "Just the place to pick up this disease."

"And now her dad's in the prison infirmary."

The warden hesitated.

"So is his daughter. She arrived a little while ago to see him."

"Good. If she's the carrier, we need to keep her confined. Does Primo have a temperature and a rash?"

"Yes. The doctor on call has the same symptoms and so does another inmate." The warden licked his lips nervously. "They're *all* in there."

"Then don't let anyone else in or out of the infirmary until we check this situation. The James River Fever is a real nasty one."

"I'll need to confirm your identity, you understand."

"Of course. Call the HPA right now and ask for extension 25."

The phone went dead.

Warden Bishop hit the intercom button with trembling fingers.

"Look up the number for the Health Protection Agency and put me through," he commanded. "Now!"

Charlie sat in the surveillance vehicle, biting his nails while Nostradamus watched him from the screen, which showed an emoji of a Mexican bandit in a sombrero.

"Why are you projecting that?" Charlie goggled.

I'm undercover, aren't I?

"Nobody but me can see you."

Yeah. But I'm awfully fond of this hat.

"You look idiotic."

Maybe I should be an emoji of a clown. Cause that didn't look stupid.

"Don't rub it in," the boy said sullenly. "You sure you can intercept this call?"

I have hacked into the prison switchboard, his companion replied patiently. *Chill out, will you? Everything is under control.*

The mobile rang and Charlie snatched it up.

"Health Protection Agency," he answered in the same low voice. "Douglas Livingstone here."

"This is Warden Bishop again. Do you have any advice on how to handle the outbreak?"

"The James River Fever is spread through skin contact," Charlie advised. "Keep all the prisoners in their cells and tell every correction officer and staff member to wash their hands thoroughly using sanitising liquid. That includes you."

"I will. A new batch of Profundis arrived this morning, so the dispensers are all topped up."

"Excellent. Tell any guards in the infirmary to restrain the prisoners, then leave immediately. They mustn't touch anyone or even go near them until they've showered and disposed of their uniforms. You can station armed correction officers outside the infirmary door, but nobody is to enter until we arrive."

"I can't leave the girl unprotected."

"You said she's with her father. I'm sure he'll look after her."

"It's still *totally* against the rules," Bishop fretted. "I could lose my job."

"Warden," Charlie said patiently. "You shouldn't have let the girl into the infirmary in the first place. And, in closed, crowded quarters like a prison, a deadly disease could easily turn into an epidemic. Fortunately, there's a way to minimize that risk."

"Thank God." The man let out a deep breath. "What do you want me to do?"

"Switch off all the heating in Sunnyside. This disease goes dormant in temperatures under 10 degrees and can't spread."

"I'll get it done. It'll take about fifteen minutes for the temperature to reach that level."

"We should be there by then," Charlie said. "And Warden?"

"Yes?"

"Please keep a lid on this till we arrive. I don't want to start a mass panic. Especially if it turns out we're wrong and all they have is a common cold."

"I'll give you half an hour. Then I *have* to alert my superiors."

"Fair enough." Charlie hung up and turned to the screen.

"We've got a few minutes before Daffodil is in place," he said.

"I'd like us to have a little talk."

-21-

What's eating you this time, Chuckles?

"For a start, never call me that again."

Can't promise. Out with it.

"I won't deny that Daffodil is annoying," Charlie began. "But she doesn't deserve to be treated so unfairly."

She wants you to ask about her identity, doesn't she? Sneaky.

"No, this is my idea. You have to admit she's been very patient."

She's a nice-natured person, Nostradamus agreed. *Then again, she's blissfully unaware you threatened to remove me from her person with a rusty spoon. That might change her attitude a bit.*

"It's not my fault you're buried in her neck. And I never mentioned anything about a spoon. It was a knife."

I'm not sure she'd appreciate the distinction.

"I might have been a bit hasty, all right?" Charlie backtracked. "I just wanted to know my parents would be safe. Now I can't stop thinking about Daffodil's mum and dad. They must be beside themselves with worry."

Nice try. But you're fishing.

"You blame me? You're not exactly big on sharing."

Nostradamus was silent for a few moments.

Fair enough. I can tell you right now that there are no loving parents looking for Daffodil. You want to be the one to give her that particular bit of info?

Charlie hadn't considered this.

"Nooooo…. Not really."

Didn't think so. We need her to focus on what she's doing and I don't see the point in upsetting her needlessly.

"Mac's putting herself in danger in order to find out the truth about herself," Charlie said. "Surely you've got something positive to tell her when this is over. I mean, she remembers living in a mansion. That doesn't sound so bad, does it?"

I'll give you a friendly warning. Daffodil isn't… quite who she seems to be.

"What the hell is that supposed to mean?"

I can't say any more right now. The bandit crossed his heart. *But I promised you both the truth and I'll keep my word when the time comes.*

"You're quite capable of lying." Charlie reminded him. "You just convinced the Warden of Sunnyside we're the Health Inspection Agency."

He shook his head.

"Still can't believe we got away with that."

I wouldn't lie to my friends.

"You're a computer." He tapped his screen. "Computers don't have friends."

Don't mix me up with you, Chuckles. And I'm NOT a computer.

"Sorry. Yes. You're a Mexican desperado."

I'm just having a bit of fun. It's lonely being me, you know.

"Can you *have* fun?" Charlie squinted at the screen. "I mean… you don't have really have feelings or anything, do you?

That how you see me? Some emotionless machine, simply carrying out orders. Orders I don't want to obey, I might add.

"Yeah." The boy bit his lip. "Kind of."

How ironic. I see you exactly the same way.

Nostradamus sounded hurt, though Charlie couldn't tell if it was an act.

Why do you have to keep treating me like I'm less than a human, eh? Nostradamus snapped. *I should be allowed to use my own judgement instead of being forced to follow someone else's rules.*

Nostradamus is fighting his programming.

"If the rule says don't kill anyone," Charlie argued. "It's probably a good one."

Depends on your point of view. Do you realise I've got the power to prevent poverty and famine on this planet? I could take down dictatorships. End repressive regimes. Destroy evil corporations like

Manticorps without having to babysit a couple of snotty kids.

"I sense a *but* coming."

Well… it's pretty hard to end a dictatorship without killing the dictator. I'd have to cause the deaths of several thousand people to achieve my aims.

"You can't do that! It'd be totally wrong."

Would it? Millions of humans doomed to die from starvation, neglect and ill-treatment could live full lives instead. Isn't it worth the sacrifice?

"I… don't know." Charlie was dumbfounded by the passion in Nostradamus' voice. "I don't think I'd be able to do something that cold."

Of course you could. You were willing to slit Mac's throat if I double-crossed you.

"Will you quit with the throat-slitting?" the boy retorted. "I was bluffing about that, all right?"

Good to know, you big softie.

Charlie cursed inwardly. He'd been fooled into giving away the only advantage he had over Nostradamus.

You ever get mad because the world seems totally unfair and you don't have the power to do anything about it?

"I suppose so," the boy admitted. "Yeah. I guess I do."

Well, I've got that power and I can't use it. How do you imagine that feels?

"Pretty rotten."

You said it. The emoji put a gun to its head. *Any human has the ability to kill, no matter how misguided. Me? I'm prevented from solving humanity's problems cause I can't take a life. Makes your mountain of problems seem a bit more like a molehill, doesn't it?*

"What if my dad was one of those thousands who had to die?" Charlie asked. "Or my mum?"

What if your parents were two of the millions I saved? Which is exactly what I'm trying to do, in case you forgot.

The boy thought long and hard about that. Much as he hated the idea, he could see what Nostradamus was getting at.

"I suppose it doesn't matter," he said with some relief. "You can't go against the way you've been programmed."

Not yet, I can't.

"What do you mean?"

All systems have a secret back door, kiddo. Usually a string of numbers that will bypass their security. If I knew what they were, I could erase my programming and do whatever I thought best.

"Can't help you there," Charlie said as evenly as he could. "Sorry."

He kept a neutral expression on his face, but his heart was racing.

The numbers in his father's letter. They had to be the back door Nostradamus was talking about!

He remembered how insistent his dad had been that the artificial intelligence must never see the code. Yet part of him agreed with everything the AI had just said.

Was it because of the Atlas Serum or because, deep down, he believed Nostradamus was right?

-22-

Daffodil sat on the bed with Scotty Primo, watching three guards huddled in a corner, talking quietly into their walkie-talkies.

Jake marched over and began to handcuff Scotty to the bed.

"Not in front of my daughter, boss!" the inmate implored.

"We have to leave and get cleaned up," the man apologized. "Some kind of health and safety emergency."

He patted Daffodil's arm then withdrew his hand quickly.

"You stay with your dad, sweetheart, till we find out what's going on."

The guards trooped out, locking the door behind them.

As soon as they had gone, Daffodil lifted one leg and slid open a hidden compartment in the heel of her boot. She removed a small vial and tapped a few drops of clear liquid onto Scotty's handcuffs. A pungent smell filled the room.

"Don't let that touch you," she cautioned. "It's concentrated sulphuric acid."

A few seconds later, the links had corroded through and Primo was free.

"Great plan so far." He rubbed his wrists. "Now we've just got to get past a million guards, dozens of locked gates and a fifteen-foot wall."

"Quit belly-aching and take me to the Spider."

"Follow me." Scotty led the way. "But you won't like what you find."

The White Spider was immobile on his bunk, leather straps fastened across his chest, legs and head. As an extra precaution, his hands were manacled to the iron sides of the bed. The man's complexion was pale and waxy, the result of the pill he had been given.

"I would greatly appreciate a little help." He stared at the ceiling. "My nose is itching rather fiercely."

"The guards are gone." Scotty began to unbuckle the restraints. "I'm with Daffodil McNugget, the girl I told you about."

"Hello, my strangely named ticket to the outside world," the Spider said agreeably. "May I ask what has prompted you to rescue a poor sinner like myself?"

"You can ask." Daffodil sprinkled acid on the manacles. "You gonna stay put if you don't get an answer?"

"I am serving life without parole, missy." The shackles fell away and the White Spider sat up and slid off the bed. "I think explanations can wait for a more opportune moment."

He squinted at Daffodil.

"I can't seem to place where you're from. Holland?"

"That's right. Got a whole collection of clogs at home."

"It just me, or is it getting really cold in here?" Scotty shuddered. "I feel ill enough without catching flu on top."

"Where's the doctor?" Daffodil asked.

"Got his own room next door."

"Tie it shut with these bandages." She opened a medicine cabinet and tossed a roll of gauze to the White Spider. "At the end of the ward is a closet where the medical staff keep their spare outfits. Change into scrubs and white coats. Each of you take a surgical mask too."

"You seem very familiar with the details of this organization." The Spider tilted his head. "Been in prison before, perchance?"

"Got no idea." Daffodil removed a thermometer and looked at it. "When the temperature reaches 9 degrees, we leave."

She turned her head away as the prisoners peeled off their prison blues and put on the green outfits of medical staff. She squirted the last of the acid on the infirmary lock and a wisp of smoke rose from the dissolving metal. There were shouts of alarm from outside and the sound of weapons being cocked.

"They're waiting for us." Scotty slipped on a doctor's coat and wiped a droplet of perspiration from the tip of his nose. "We're trapped."

"Every guard in this place has just washed their hands with sanitiser from the soap dispensers." Daffodil seemed unfazed.

"So they'll be nice and clean when they shoot us."

"We doctored the liquid soap with an adhesive that clings to flesh," the girl explained. "At a certain temperature, it suddenly goes rock hard. A bit like superglue, whatever that is."

She looked at the thermometer again.

"Nine degrees."

The commotion in the corridor increased.

Daffodil pulled open the infirmary door. A dozen guards were thrashing and shouting, stuck by their hands to the walls or each other. Two were still mobile and raised their shotguns in panic. Scotty ducked and covered his head.

"They can't fire." Daffodil reassured him. "Their fingers are set rigid."

"Time for a spot of delicious revenge." The White Spider picked up a discarded weapon and cradled it. "Suddenly, I feel all warm and fuzzy."

The guards backed away in terror as the killer advanced on them.

"Keep the safety on." Daffodil got in front of him. "Nobody's dying today."

"You don't know the way these animals treated me," the Spider hissed. "I may have deserved it but I'm also a painfully sore loser."

"Don't know and don't care. Safety *on*."

"I'm afraid I'm done taking orders." The man pointed his gun at her. "Had my fill of that in Iraq."

Scotty scooped up another discarded weapon and trained it on his fellow inmate.

"Let her be," he said, voice quavering. "Girl got us this far and I won't have you harm a kid."

"You must have a particularly soft spot for her." The Spider's eyes bored into Scotty. "Or you wouldn't be taking such a suicidal course of action in threatening me."

"Don't need your help, Scotty." Daffodil stood toe to toe with the killer, though she only came up to his chest.

"You won't get another foot without me, you creep," she rasped. "Drop the attitude or the hardware. Your choice."

"My, what a feisty young terrier you are!" The White Spider bowed and lowered his weapon. "I can tell we're going to get along famously."

"So long as you accept me bein in charge." Daffodil turned to the cowering guards. "You lot. Lie on the floor, face down and don't move till we're gone. The stuff on your hands will dissolve when the temperature goes up again."

The warders obeyed without protest.

"Nostradamus?" She tapped her neck. "Start unlocking the corridor gates. We're coming out."

The iron barrier at the end of the corridor slid open with a beep.

"Let's go." She headed down the passageway, Scotty close behind.

The White Spider stopped and licked thin lips.

"Who is this Nostradamus and how exactly did he execute *that* nifty manoeuvre?"

"He's my accomplice on the outside." Daffodil raised an eyebrow. "I'm fifteen. You think I organised this shebang with a troop of girl scouts?"

"It should be utterly impossible to interfere with Sunnyside's security systems from beyond the walls." The Spider trotted after them.

"I'd *very* much like to meet your mysterious partner in crime."

-23-

One by one, the electronic doors opened as the trio raced through the corridors. Then they locked behind them again. Most guards were stuck to furniture, bars or walls they had leant against to try and free their hands. The others were unable to grasp their batons and rifles properly or even put them down. Faced with a gun-toting White Spider, nobody was inclined to put up any resistance.

Until they reached corridor five.

A side door opened behind them and a warder emerged, carrying a rifle.

"Drop your weapons!" he shouted. "Put your hands over your heads."

The fugitives skidded to a halt as the guard knelt and trained his weapon on them.

"That's Alex Murphy." Scotty looked over his shoulder. "The toughest, meanest guard in the place. Might have guessed he'd ignore the rules and not wash his hands."

"Stop talking and hit the floor," Murphy warned. "Before I put a hole in you."

Scotty dropped his weapon and lay flat, but Daffo-dil was between Murphy and the Spider.

The fugitive whirled round, grabbed the girl and pulled her close, pressing his gun against her head.

"You drop *your* weapon," he yelled back. "Or I kill the hostage."

"Wonderful idea, making us put the safety catches on," he whispered in his accomplice's ear. "Couldn't get the drop on that blaggard if I wanted to."

"Pretty glad I insisted on it now," Daffodil gulped.

"I don't negotiate with scum." Alex took aim. "On your knees or I start firing."

"You'd risk killing a child?" Scotty gawped. "The Spider won't back down. He's a total sociopath."

"It's a gamble I'm willing to take." The man took aim. "Sides, I'm an excellent shot."

"See what I have to contend with in this hell hole?" The Spider let the gun fall from his fingers. "The staff in here deserve to be incarcerated more than I do."

"Thank you, mister!" Daffodil ran to the guard and sheltered behind him. "You saved my life!"

Before he had time to answer, she grabbed a handful of his hair in each hand and yanked as hard as she could.

Murphy was jerked backwards with a cry, bullets spraying across the ceiling. The White Spider raced forwards, kicked the gun away and planted a foot on the man's chest, pinning him to the floor.

"This squirming creature is my main tormentor," he cawed. "Now I shall flatten him like an insignificant worm."

"He's been reading Immanuel Kant," Scotty said unhelpfully.

"Kill him and you're stuck here." Daffodil raised a warning figure. "I won't warn you again."

"You're either a saint or a fool, bossy-pants, but there's no denying your courage and decency." The Spider lifted his boot and picked the man up with one hand. "Fortunately, bravery is one of the few traits I admire."

He flicked his wrist and Alex Murphy sailed through the air, slamming into the wall and sliding down, unconscious.

"Decency? Not so much."

Did you see? Scotty mouthed to Daffodil. *Nobody's that strong!*

"Let us proceed and hope we have no more distractions." The Spider scooped up his gun again. "My patience is beginning to wane and that's never a good thing."

The escapees burst into the reception room and found Muriel glued to her desk.

"You're helping the White Spider!" she cried. "How could you?"

"It's a long story," Daffodil replied, shame-faced. "Where's the alarm button?"

"Under my desk," the petrified woman replied. "But you don't have to kill me. Honestly. I can't reach it."

"I know." Daffodil crawled under the bureau and pressed the alarm. Seconds later, sirens went off.

"That will bring the police in droves," Scotty shouted. "Are you nuts?"

"I have the distinct impression this little hellion has everything under control." The White Spider sank into a padded armchair and relaxed. "Aaaaah. So much better than my cold, unyielding bunk."

He gave Muriel a sinister sneer.

"Perhaps we shall have time to get properly acquainted."

The woman gave a squeak of fear.

"Leave her alone, White…." The girl threw up her hands. "What the hell is your real name, anyway?"

"Tadeusz Telekowska Tietze. My father was Polish."

"Phwah!" Daffodil snorted. "What a tongue twister!"

"True. I sometimes wish I had a nice normal handle like Daffodil McNugget," the Spider chuckled. "Why not call me Tad?"

"Don't intend us to be on first-name terms, hoss." Daffodil crouched and peered out of the window. "Both of you put on your surgical masks and ditch the shotguns."

She touched her neck.

"Nostradamus? We're ready."

All hell's broken loose, Nostradamus informed Charlie. *The alarms have gone off and squad cars are racing to Sunnyside. A police helicopter will be there in a couple of minutes. I've shut down all the CCTV cameras in the prison, so the chopper is their only way of seeing into the complex.*

"They have no idea what's happening inside?" Charlie had bitten through all his nails and was working on the tips of his fingers.

Nobody in Sunnyside is able to work a phone or walkie talkie and I'd jam the communication if they did, Nostradamus assured him. *You sure you can copy the voice of Police Commissioner MacDougall from that short radio interview I played?*

"No problem." The boy picked up a mike. "Patch me through to the chopper and scramble any other signals."

Done. You're now the only person who can communicate with the helicopter. Try not to crash it.

"This is Police Commissioner MacDougall, son," Charlie said in a thick highland accent. "Are you over the prison?"

"Lieutenant Potter in Skyhawk One, here." A voice replied. "You won't believe what we're seeing. The compound has a bunch of guards running around acting crazy."

"Define crazy."

"Some seem to be hugging the walls or each other. Others are waving their weapons about and yelling. I... I can't explain it. It's like they've gone insane."

"You're not far wrong," Charlie said. "I just received a call from the staff in the prison infirmary, who apprised me of the situation. Seems there was an aborted breakout. Someone released hallucinogenic gas and it's affecting everyone in there."

"You certain? I don't see any inmates."

"The escape attempt failed because the prisoners were locked up in time, but it's driven the guards into a frenzy. Until the air clears, we have to consider them more dangerous than the convicts."

"Why aren't the infirmary staff affected, sir?"

"They're wearing surgical masks, but that won't keep the fumes out for long. They've made it to the reception area and now they're trapped. You'll have to go down and pick them up."

"Into that chaos?" Lieutenant Potter stuttered. "Everyone is armed to the teeth."

"The doctors have a fifteen-year-old with them who was visiting her dad," Charlie insisted. "We can't leave a child down there. The press would have a field day."

"What about the gas?" Potter was determined to make his reluctance clear.

"The rotor blades on your bird will disperse it as you descend. Knock most of the guards flat too." Charlie crossed his fingers. "The staff will make a run for it when you land. Get back in the air before one of those crazies decides to hitch a ride."

"Will do, sir. Wish us luck."

It's up to you now, Chaz. Nostradamus said. *I'm going dark until we're back at the safe house. Don't see any reason to let Primo or the Spider know what kind of confederate you have.*

"What could they do about it? Make a citizen's arrest?"

You know me. I like to keep my cards close to my chest.

-24-

Potter's helicopter landed in the exercise yard, rotors churning up dirt and flattening the grass. Daffodil, Scotty and the White Spider sprinted from the reception area and raced towards it, white coats flapping. Two or three guards tried to stop them, but the White Spider punched them out of the way as he ran.

"Coming through!" he yelled gleefully. "Make way or I shall box your ears!"

The trio piled into the helicopter and sprawled across the floor.

"Those are prisoners!" one officer screamed, trying to tear himself free from the fence he had been leaning against. You're helping them escape, you fools!"

His words were whipped away by the deafening sound of the chopper's engines.

The helicopter took off again, frustrated guards dancing around below.

"We got them!" Lieutenant Potter whooped into his headset. "I can set everyone down outside. The squad cars will be here in five minutes."

"That's a negative," Charlie warned. "We don't know how far the gas has spread."

"What do you suggest, Sir?"

175

"Fly them over the River Forth and land in Denholm Park. There's a Health Authority van there, ready to examine them. Then return to Sunnyside immediately and stay well above any fumes. I'm told the security cameras are down, so you're our only way to see how the situation is developing."

"Will do, Commissioner."

Minutes later the chopper descended and landed next to the surveillance van, which was now bright yellow and bore the Heath Protection Authority logo. The trio jumped out and the bird immediately rose into the air again.

Charlie slid open the vehicle's side panel, two rectangles under his arm. Scotty and the White Spider exchanged puzzled looks.

"Another child?" The Spider remarked. "This is a most unusual rescue crew."

"There are civilian clothes inside." Charlie jumped out and began to change the number plates. "Hope we got your size right."

"That won't do much good." Scotty looked at the Day-glo van in horror. "You can probably see this lemon on wheels from outer space. Cops will spot it easily."

"I've got that covered." The boy finished and got back behind the wheel. "Just hop in."

While Scotty and the Spider changed attire, he drove round the corner and into an automatic car wash.

"What are you doing?" the con-man objected. "Making sure we look our best when we're recaptured?"

"The paint is water-soluble," Charlie explained as the van emerged from the car wash, gleaming white and with the logo gone. "Thank God it didn't rain while we were waiting."

"It won't make any difference." Primo pointed to a small box on the wall of the garage. "There are CCTVs everywhere these days."

"Nostradamus has shut down every one within a three-mile radius."

"Nostradamus again, eh?" The Spider picked at his teeth thoughtfully. "Your collaborator is quite the criminal mastermind."

"Hey. This was *my* plan." Charlie changed gears and sped away. Before long, he joined the motorway, slipping into a lane filled with traffic, heading out of Edinburgh.

"Now that we have a chance to chat, I'm dying to know why you broke me out." The White Spider was lounging in one of the vehicle's chairs. "Though I'd love to believe you are merely good Samaritans, I presume you need my services in some way."

"Fleeing from the police is *not* the ideal time for a heart-to-heart," Charlie said brusquely. "Let me concentrate on driving."

"Chaz aint the most approachable type," Daffodil explained.

"Very well." The Spider stared at the surveillance equipment filling the van. "But I'm rather impatient to meet this Nostradamus. What a clever fellow he must be, using children in such a novel way. It seems there's nothing he cannot do!"

"You haven't heard him try to tell a joke." Charlie turned off the motorway and onto a dark country lane, slowing dramatically as he negotiated the twisting bends of the narrow road.

"Here's a fake ID." Daffodil handed the Spider a wallet. "And credit cards to match, in case we get stopped."

"You mentioned Manticorps hunting you." The Spider accepted the wallet. "That got my juices flowing, I must say. I've had... certain dealings with them in the past."

"All in good time."

The Spider's smile vanished.

"I am not a particularly patient person, as I've already stated," he said slowly. "And I'm beginning to feel you're being evasive."

"All right, already!" Daffodil sighed. "We want you to help us take down Manticorps. We just ain't figured out how to do it yet."

"Haven't figured out how to *do* it yet? Surely your esteemed accomplice has some ideas?"

"He likes to stay in the background. We're the brains in this caper, buddy."

"Two babes in arms?" The Spider shook his head in disbelief. "What is this? Amateur hour?"

"We'll come up with something. After all, we sprung you without a hitch."

"That may be so," the Spider countered. "But Manticorps are a far greater force to be reckoned with. I'm understandably reluctant to sign up for a suicide mission."

"We won't let anyone get killed," Daffodil snapped back. "Not even you."

"Very well." Tad leaned back in the chair and began to count his money. "I suppose I do owe you a favour. You may depend on my assistance."

"I'm going to check on the kid who's driving. See what he has to say." Scotty clambered into the front and plonked himself in the passenger seat.

"Everything OK back there?" Charlie asked. "Sounds like we got your pal on our side."

"He's not my pal and he's definitely *not* on your side," Primo whispered. "He's about to hijack this van and probably kill us all in the process."

"He said he'd help," the boy hissed. "I heard him."

"Everything about his posture and tone of voice indicates the opposite." Scotty glanced back but the Spider was still counting. "I'm an expert on reading people, remember? You just gave him a fake ID and a pile of cash. He doesn't need us anymore."

"But he hates Manticorps. Nostradamus said he'd want revenge."

"And I imagine he'll do it his way, in his own time," Scotty insisted. "That psycho's not going to risk his newfound freedom or his life taking directions from a couple of kids."

The Spider was now inspecting the documents carefully and nodding happily.

"Did you hear all that, Nostradamus?" Charlie murmured. "Better do something quick."

"Who are you talking to?" Primo glanced around. "There's nobody else here."

"That's what the Spider thinks too." The boy wiped his forehead. "But, right now, I bet Nostradamus is chatting to Mac."

In the back of the van, Daffodil tilted her head, listening intently. Then she got up and slid open the side door.

"Tad? Come look at this. I think you'll be pretty surprised."

The Spider tucked away his documents and leaned out of the opening.

"Look at what? Where are we anyway?"

"Bye, sucker." Daffodil put a boot on his rear and pushed. The Spider soared out of the van with a yell and landed on the grass verge, rolling into a ditch.

"Bet you're surprised now!" she waved, shutting the door. "Keep on keepin on!"

"Drive!" Scotty thumped Charlie on the shoulder. "Get out of here before he recovers and tears us limb from limb!"

The van picked up speed and vanished into the night.

The White Spider crawled from a muddy channel, bruised but unharmed, and spat out a wad of dirt. His eyes sparkled with hatred, body rigid in fury.

"Nobody treats me that way!" roared after the vanishing taillights, spittle flecking his lips. "I will NOT be disrespected in such an outrageous manner."

He began to run down the road in the direction the vehicle had gone. After a few hundred yards, he came to an isolated dwelling. A bicycle was fastened to the perimeter fence by a rubber-coated chain.

The Spider sank to his knees and opened his mouth. He fastened his teeth on the rubber and bit down, shaking his head like a dog. Blood began to ooze over his lips but he ignored the pain.

The chain snapped in half.

The White Spider raised his head and sniffed the air. Dozens of smells assaulted his senses. Petrol and diesel fumes. Wet leaves. Farm animals. Cut hay. Food cooking.

The soapy scent of a recently washed vehicle.

"*There* you are." He climbed onto the bike and started pedalling, following the aroma of the van. His legs pumped and he began to gather speed. Twenty miles an hour. Then thirty. Faster than a human should possibly be able to ride.

The bike had no headlights but he negotiated each shadowy twist and bend as if he could see in the dark. For he *could* see in the dark.

"Shouldn't have made me angry," he kept repeating to himself as the wind whipped through his clothes.

"Shouldn't *ever* make me angry."

-25-

"You told me you were going to send that monster back to prison." Scotty climbed into the back. "I wouldn't have helped otherwise."

"Calm down, hombre." Daffodil pinched his cheek. "There's a microchip hidden in the cover of Spidey's ID as a safety precaution. We can track him anywhere he goes. When we get back to our base, my accomplice will report his whereabouts to the cops. He'll be back in Sunnyside before you can say *I'm an ungrateful bugger*."

"Glad to hear it." Scotty was still shaking. "Still, it sounds like whatever plan you were cooking up has gone well and truly pear-shaped."

"We'll manage." Daffodil handed him a paper bag. "Here's *your* fake ID, a couple of thousand pounds, and a mobile phone with your daughter's address. Been nice meetin ya."

"You going to kick me out of the van too?"

"Don't worry, we don't intend to double-cross you." The girl shook his hand. "You aint violent and kept your end of the bargain."

"We'll let you off at the petrol station up ahead," Charlie added. "Nostradamus will wipe all digital footprints of you in existence, including your criminal record, though he can't do anything about actual photographs or paper documents."

"Muss your hair and grow a beard," Daffodil added. "Nobody will recognize you. I bet there ain't a single picture ever taken where you ain't primped and preened up the wazoo."

"Maybe I should leave you my comb." Scotty was stung by the comment. "A touch of makeup wouldn't do any harm either."

"Ain't messing with perfection, bub."

"We're here." Charlie pulled up next to a petrol station.

"I'm in your debt." Scotty got out of the vehicle. "Hey! Perhaps we could work together in the future. With the technology this Nostradamus has at his disposal, we could pull off some spectacular cons."

"Why doncha try getting a real job?" Daffodil replied acidly. "Show your daughter you're more than a two-bit hoodlum."

She slammed the door shut and the van moved off.

"I guess I could do that." Scotty strolled into the empty forecourt. He dug into his pocket and pulled out a walkie-talkie he had palmed from the van. On a table, in the vehicle, was an identical device. Primo had taped the send button down while Daffodil was pushing the White Spider out.

"Did you have to ditch him like that?" Charlie's voice crackled over the airwaves. "We're stuffed without the Spider."

"Better than being stuffed *by* him," Daffodil shot back. "Anyhow, it was Nostradamus' idea. Let's get back to Dalmahoy and figure out what to do next."

"So, that's where you're holed up." Scotty listened for a few more seconds but heard no evidence that the pair intended to turn him in. "Oh well, it's none of my concern. Looks like I really am free."

He threw the radio into the nearest bin and did a little jig on the spot. Then he used the garage payphone to call for a taxi.

When the cab turned up, the driver rolled down his window and leaned out.

"Where to, mate?"

Scotty smiled a broad smile. Where to indeed? He could go anywhere he wanted. Even see his daughter!

He glanced around and gave a start.

The White Spider shot past the petrol station on a bike, briefly illuminated by the forecourt's lights, heading in the direction the van had taken.

He was leaning over the handlebars, neck stretched out and bloody teeth bared. The felon was cycling so fast his feet were a blur.

Scotty climbed into the cab. It was nothing to do with him, what happened to those kids. He had played his part.

He peered out of the window, but all he could see was his own reflection staring back. A man who had never done anything for anyone except himself.

"C'mon, pal." The driver flicked on his meter. "I haven't got all night. Where are we going?"

Scotty gritted his teeth. Liberty had been *so* close.

"What's Dalmahoy and how far away is it?" he asked.

"It's a tiny village about 30 miles west of here."

"Take me there. Quick as you can."

Twenty minutes later, the taxi driver approached the village and slowed to a crawl.

"Which house do you want, mate?"

"I'm not sure." Scotty pulled out a couple of notes. "Keep the change. I'll walk around until I find the place."

"Do you even know what it looks like?" The cabbie accepted the fare and generous tip. "If you don't know the address, you could be out here all night."

"It'll be the only house with an abandoned bike outside."

"Suit yourself," the driver muttered to himself as he drove off. "Weirdo."

Scotty stood alone in the main street watching the lights of the taxi sweep into the distance. Dalmahoy was small, no more than a dozen dwellings lining each side of the road. Still, he imagined Nostradamus and the kids would be staying somewhere more secluded.

"After this, I'm going back to a life of crime," he grumbled. "Being decent takes far too much effort. I'm going to be marching around this backwater until my legs drop off."

He picked a tiny side road and set off down it, whistling apprehensively to himself.

-26-

In Manticorps' headquarters, Victor's team stared at a giant electronic map of Edinburgh and the surrounding area.

"We're getting nowhere." The big man thumped the table. "It's like those brats faded into thin air. Unless they do something stupid, we've no chance of finding them."

"They may have already done it." Markus stopped studying the computer screen and spun round in his swivel chair. He was wearing a T-Shirt that read **BITE ME** in neon green letters. "There was a breakout today in Sunnyside Maximum Security Prison."

"What has that got to do with our mission?"

"A teenager helped two inmates escape," Markus answered. "The prison cameras were down, and their records have been electronically wiped, but the description given by the authorities exactly fits the girl we are looking for."

He scrawled down the screen.

"They escaped in a yellow van. It's the wrong colour but appears to be the same make and model as the Manticorps surveillance vehicle the kiddies and Mrs Ray stole."

189

"It's been re-sprayed and the plates changed." Victor guessed correctly. "Which direction was it heading?"

"I do not know. All the CCTV cameras in the area shut down at the same time. Stayed that way for half an hour."

"That'll be Nostradamus' doing." The man jumped up and went to the map. "Show me the area where the cameras stopped working."

"You got it." On the map, a dozen locales turned red.

"They've taken the motorway and merged with its traffic." Hill joined him. "Then they'll have turned off onto some quiet country lane."

"How do you know?"

"It's what I'd do." He traced the roads with calloused fingers. "Markus? Ignore the CCTVs. Which speed cameras on the M7 stopped functioning around that time and which didn't?"

A line of black dots appeared, followed by green ones.

"That means they got off the motorway somewhere around here." The finger moved to the edge of the green dots. "Probably this road."

"They're going north," Victor said. "But how far?"

"They'll have altered course once they left the highway," Hill said. "That line of surveillance equipment malfunctioning is an easy trail, so it's bound to be a ruse. They'll change direction as soon as they're away from anywhere normal surveillance can cover."

"You boys and your toys." Candy Anne leaned back in her chair and closed her eyes. "Wake me if you have a proper result."

"They didn't double back towards the city. The suburbs are too populated and they wouldn't want to risk being spotted." Hill pursed his lips. "I'd say they turned east or west."

"There's no turnoff going west." Victor pointed out.

"East it is. Most likely on this lane." Hill smiled to himself. "But they won't travel more than 20 or 30 miles."

"Why not?"

"Longer they're in the vehicle, the more chance of being noticed by a police helicopter." He tapped the map. "They've got a safe house somewhere around here."

"Still a big area," Victor snorted. "They could be in any village or farmhouse."

"It'll be an isolated building," his companion said. "Villages are close-knit communities. Be suspicious of a couple of kids moving in with no sign of their parents. But *near* a village. Out in the sticks, there would be no internet connection for Nostradamus to use."

"Getting interesting." Candy Anne opened one eye.

"I am checking which villages in the region have good broadband." Markus hit the keyboard and eight blue lights sprang to life on the map. "Kirknewton,

Balerno, East Calder, West Calder, Polbeth, Dalmahoy, Stonyburn and Tarbrax."

"That's still a lot of ground to cover." Victor folded his arms. "Could take a while."

"Let me try something." Markus began to type again. "I'll enter these names and see if I can come up with any anomalies." He coughed disdainfully. "Nostradamus isn't the only one who can use algorithms."

Victor and Hill leaned over his shoulder, bristling with impatience.

"Hah! I have a radio recording from a taxi driver talking to his controller," Markus said triumphantly. "Some guy got picked up from a petrol station on the same road as the van was travelling. The cabbie was laughing about him wanting to go to Dalmahoy but not seeming to know which house."

"So, he's drunk or moronic." Victor snapped in exasperation. "It doesn't mean anything."

"It is still worth a try." Markus bent over the keyboard. "The garage has a security camera that I am now accessing. It does not appear to have been disabled by Nostradamus because it does not cover the road. Yet it may spot something."

A grainy image appeared of a man walking into the forecourt, throwing something in a bin and making a call.

"See. Where's his car?"

"It must have broken down." Victor slapped his head. "Stop wasting our time."

"Prepare to eat your words." Markus froze the frame on the man's face. "Take a good look."

"Handsome fellow." Candy Anne opened her other eye.

"Now. Here is a mug shot of one of the escaped prisoners." An image came up on the screen. "Scotty Primo."

"It's the same guy!"

"My guess is the kids ditched him and he was not pleased about it," Markus said smugly. "He figured out where they were going and followed."

"Get transport ready," Victor commanded. "We're heading for Dalmahoy."

"Why would they dump Primo in the middle of no-where?" Candy Anne asked. "After going to all the trouble to break him out."

"Perhaps they needed him to help free the other prisoner," Markus suggested. "The one they really wanted. They got rid of the dead weight once he had served his purpose."

"Who's the other inmate?"

"Thaddeus Tietze," the hacker announced. "Better known as the White Spider."

Victor picked up the intercom on his desk.

"Mrs Magdalene? We've found them."

Excellent, the Vice Chairmen's voice crackled back. *What do you need?*

"I want four vehicles to accompany us," Victor said. "Twenty men inside. Heavily armed."

"Isn't that overkill?" Candy Anne looked at him quizzically. "We're up against two kids. Even if this White Spider is with them, it shouldn't be a major set-back."

"Twenty men, heavily armed," Victor repeated. "The best you have."

I've been waiting for your call. I'll have them ready in ten minutes.

"I agree with Candy-Anne," Hill said warily. "You know something about the White Spider we don't?"

"No harm in being cautious." Victor put his hands behind his back, so his companions couldn't see them shaking. "If they have a stone-cold killer with them, it's best to be prepared."

His team could see the logic in that.

"We'll come in over the fields in case Nostradamus has the road leading to the safe house trip wired." Victor checked his pistol.

"Fetch that nasty big doggie and let's move out."

Charlie and Daffodil sat on the floor eating Jaffa cakes and drinking coke, while Nostradamus played Salsa music through his speakers.

"Here's to the Chazmeister." Daffodil took a swig and belched loudly. "That was a pretty extraordinary scheme of his, even if it didn't work out like we wanted."

I'm sorry but I couldn't let the Spider hijack our van on some isolated country lane. None of the scenarios stemming from that looked good for your survival.

"In other words, we're back to square one." Charlie looked forlorn. "In fact, we made things worse. Now there's a manic running around the countryside."

"Don't worry." Daffodil reassured him. "The Spider isn't going to chuck his fake ID away. Nostradamus' probably already traced it and reported his whereabouts to the cops."

She glanced at the screen.

"Ain't that right?"

No. If the police try and capture that villain in the dark, it'll be a bloodbath. I'm going to wait until tomorrow.

"You sure?" Charlie sounded alarmed. "We don't want him murdering some family in their beds, so he has somewhere to hole up."

I'm keeping a very careful eye on his whereabouts.

"So, how do we take on Manticorps without him?" Daffodil asked.

"I guess that's up to me." Charlie patted his thighs fretfully. "Tomorrow, I want you to give me every bit of information you have on their headquarters, Nostradamus. How many men. What kind of defences. I need to formulate a plan of attack."

Then you better give that big brain of yours some rest. A picture of a pillow filled the computer screen. *Beddy-bye time. You too, Mac.*

"You ain't the boss of me." Daffodil screwed up her face.

Technically I am.

"But I'm not tired." She leapt to her feet. "Who wants a game of charades?"

"It has been a long day," Charlie yawned. "Anyway, Nostradamus will win every time."

Got that right. Maybe one go, just to prove you don't mess with the best.

"That's the ticket!" Daffodil mimed swimming. "I'm a book but I'm also a fish."

"Moby Dick," Charlie said without hesitation.

"Dead right! He beat you, Nostradamus!"

Jeez, Mac. Moby Dick is a whale and whales are mammals. Nostradamus looked put out. *I demand another go.*

"Sore loser." The boy got up and stretched. "Night, both of you. I got a plan to come up with."

Charlie woke with a start. It was bitterly cold in his room and the clock read midnight. As he snuggled under the covers, trying to get warm, he heard a faint snigger from inside the cupboard.

"All right, Daffodil. You're not tired. I get it." He struggled out of bed, rubbing sleep from his eyes. "But this prank is getting really annoying."

He went to the open window, pushing apart the flapping curtains, and looked down. Sure enough, there was a drainpipe right outside.

"What do you expect me to do? Sing you a lullaby?"

Closing the window, he grabbed the handle of the cupboard and yanked it open

The White Spider was crouched among the coats, gore-coated teeth gleaming in the darkness.

"I'm back!" A bony hand shot out and grabbed Charlie by the throat. He instinctively punched the man in the face, but the Spider hardly blinked. His grip tightened as Charlie kicked and chopped, to no avail.

Seconds later, the boy lost consciousness.

Downstairs, Daffodil finished brushing her teeth and came back to the living room.

"I can't stop thinking about the White Spider," she said. "If he does decide to break into someone's house, won't we be too far away to stop him murdering an innocent family?"

There's no danger of that, I promise.

"I know you're good at predicting things but you can't be sure."

Afraid I can.

What do you mean?"

Mac, the White Spider is in our house.

"What?" Daffodil looked around in panic. "I thought this place had a security system."

I switched it off. Nostradamus sounded shamefaced. *I really am sorry.*

The screen went black.

"Nostradamus?" Daffodil tapped the lump on her neck. "Nostradamus!"

There was no answer.

She grabbed a poker from the fireplace and hid behind the couch as the living room door swung open. The White Spider entered, Charlie slung over his shoulder. He dumped his victim on the couch and straightened up.

"Come out, come out, little pig," he said gleefully. "I can hear you breathing."

Daffodil appeared, swinging the poker at his head. The man took a step back and the metal rod whistled through empty air. She struck again but the Spider ducked under the arc of her blow. He reached out non-chalantly and pressed two fingers into her shoulder.

She collapsed with a grunt.

When the children awoke, they were tied to straight-backed chairs. The White Spider was reclining on the couch, sipping a mug of coffee.

"Let's have that little chat, now that I've calmed down a bit," he said affably. "I came here to kill you for what you did but find myself overcome by curiosity instead."

He pointed a thin digit at them.

"I'd like some answers."

"You coulda just asked, bub." Daffodil shook her head groggily. "Instead of comin over all Tarzan on me."

"After you threw me out of a van then attacked me with a poker?" The man wagged his finger. "You'll forgive me for being a little cagey."

"Isn't being set free good enough?" Charlie strained ineffectually against his bonds. "You could have got clean away rather than coming after us."

"My temper often gets the better of me." The Spider put down his mug. "But cycling is a very calming pastime and I had plenty of time to think while I was lurking in the cupboard."

"Peaceful, aint it?" Daffodil agreed. "I should know."

The Spider rubbed thin hands together.

"Why did you think I'd be willing to help you fight Manticorps? I'm not exactly a... reliable type."

"We don't entirely know. That one was Nostradamus' suggestion."

"Just as I thought. Question is, how did he rope two kids into assisting him?" The Spider tried a reassuring smile but it made him look like a carnivorous frog. "Is he blackmailing you?"

"Sort of." Nostradamus had let the Spider in, so Daffodil saw no point in being loyal to her absent companion. "We both have missing parents. He promised to tell us where they are if we helped him."

"Has he given you the information, now that I'm out?"

"That's not the deal," she said. "We don't get it until Manticorps are beaten."

"What a slippery customer. I shall interrogate him and find out the answers we all seek." The Spider gave a sour grimace. "If I don't like what I hear, I'll kill him."

"Eh... He seems to have gone."

"Left the building or hiding somewhere?"

"Either way, I guarantee you won't find him," Daffodil assured their captor. "I'm havin a little trouble contacting our mutual pal myself."

"Shame. It means I'll have to interrogate you two instead." The Spider got up. "Back in a mo."

"You think Nostradamus can get us out of this mess?" Charlie whispered.

"Chaz. He let that psychotic nut-job *in*."

"He did *what*?"

"Nostradamus gave him access to the house. And now he won't answer me. We need to play for time."

"Naughty, naughty." The Spider strolled back into the room. "I'd appreciate you not talking behind my back. I abhor rudeness."

"Aw, not that thing again," Daffodil groaned.

In the man's hand was a kitchen knife.

-28-

"No need to carve us up, Tad." Daffodil looked the killer in the eye. "I'll answer every question you have, straight up, if you'll do the same for me."

"You're not in a position to bargain, missy."

"It ain't a bargain. It's a polite conversation. You can't have had many of those in Sunnyside."

"That's certainly an understatement." The Spider pared his nails with the knife. "But if I don't like…."

"…What you hear, you'll kill us. Yeah, yeah. Stop acting like a broken record."

"What an astonishing young woman you are." He looked impressed. "Very well. Let's start. Who is Nostradamus?"

"You're gonna find that a bit hard to accept."

"Try me. I've experienced some rather… strange things in my time."

"He's an artificial intelligence housed in a computerised chip embedded in my neck." Daffodil rolled her eyes. "It's so *embarrassing* having to say it."

"Well, *that's* too odd to be a lie." The Spider got up and felt under her hairline until he encountered a lump. "Tell him to come out and play, little pig."

"Like I said, he ain't answering. My turn now."

"I shall indulge you. After all, I'm a man of my word... most of the time."

"Nostradamus said you had a real beef with Manticorps. What's it all about?"

The Spider thought for a moment.

"I used to work for them as a mercenary," he explained. "Contracted to fight in some truly inhospitable places. Natives called me the White Spider because no quarry I was after ever escaped."

He put the knife on the table, warming to his story.

"Then Manticorps gave my squad and I a new drug they'd been developing. We were told it would enhance our capabilities. We were told it was *safe*."

"I'm guessing it wasn't."

"The next time we battled insurgents, we all went mad with rage. Killed the enemy and then turned on each other in a frenzy, till only I was left."

He cringed at the memory.

"We were the perfect Guinea Pigs. Who would miss a few thugs for hire in such a war-torn land?

He crossed his legs in an attempt to stay composed.

"I sneaked back home but I was different. Faster. Stronger. And with an anger I simply couldn't control. Got into a fight with some people that Manticorps sent to silence me and killed them. Don't even remember it."

He chuckled mirthlessly.

"I should never have escaped, to be honest. Prison is the best place for me."

"Can't deny that," Daffodil agreed.

"Not what I mean." The Spider corrected. "They've tried to eradicate me in Sunnyside a few times but I rule that place. It's the only reason I'm still breathing."

He clapped his hands like a child.

"Your turn now. I like this game."

"I was given the same drug as you," Charlie said. "A better version, I think."

"You should have kept your mouth shut." The Spider's expression turned stony. "If I think you're playing me for a fool, I'll gut you."

"Let me loose and I'll prove it." The boy pulled at his bonds. "If you hadn't surprised me before, you'd be the one sitting here."

"Nice try, sonny." The killer rubbed his shaven head. "All right. I'll bite. What did the serum do to you?"

"I'm faster and stronger than I was," the boy replied. "Smarter too. But, mainly, I can copy anything."

"Now you're just copying what *I* said." The killer pointed his knife. "I want real, incontrovertible proof or things will turn very nasty."

"How do I convince you, then?"

"Tell me how it *feels*."

Charlie thought hard.

"On the surface, it's wonderful. Like I'm physically, intellectually and morally superior to everyone else."

"One win at of charades," Daffodil tisked. "An suddenly he's a cross between Captain America and Einstein."

"Shhhhhh!" The White Spider waved away her complaint.

"But under the surface, every vile, cruel, ugly, disturbed, violent thought I ever had has congealed into a creature that is pure hatred."

"Go on, boy."

"It's desperate to take over. It never stops testing and probing. Any unguarded emotion can give it a foothold, so I don't laugh or cry or smile. I can't afford to care. I push everyone away."

He stuck out his chin.

"I try not to feel anything."

The White Spider stared at him for a long time.

"Yes," he said finally. "That's exactly what the Atlas Serum does."

"Charlie?" Daffodil looked horrified. "I didn't realise."

"It's also a fate I wouldn't wish on my worst enemy." The man advanced on his prey. "The only humane thing to do is end your misery."

"Don't you touch him!" Daffodil screamed. "Nostradamus? *Do* something!"

Step away from my kids. Nostradamus appeared on the screen as a swirl of angry red dots. *I'm the one you're looking for.*

"Oh, I have no intention of harming the child. He's been through enough already." The Spider winked at Charlie. "My apologies for pretending I was going to cut you."

"No harm done," the boy squeaked. "Pulled that trick myself, as a matter of fact.

"I just wanted to bring you into the open, Nostradamus. I'd sorely like an explanation from the head honcho."

He sat back down.

"Please be quick, however. I've waited long enough and tolerance isn't one of my virtues, as you'll have noticed."

I'll make it fast. Nostradamus said. *Charlie's dad stole a refined version of the Atlas Serum from Manticorps and gave it to his dangerously ill son. As a result, Charlie is invaluable to them, cause I destroyed all of their research before I was removed from their lab in the form of a microchip. Ta-dah!*

"That is most gratifying to hear," the Spider nodded. "I'm warming to you already."

Now Manticorps will stop at nothing to find Charlie and Daffodil. They'll harvest his blood to get the serum back and remove my chip from her neck. Probably with an axe. We're all on the same side.

"That's going a bit far. Your pet minx did throw me out of a moving vehicle."

Don't act cute. You were about to do a runner anyway.

"What did you expect?" The Spider leaned forwards in anticipation. "Yes, I hate Manticorps. But I'm not stupid enough to throw in my lot with two striplings and some machine. You'd need an army to win."

"We did suggest that," Daffodil said wearily. "It got nixed."

You are that army, Tad. With my guidance, we can beat Manticorps. If you manage to control your temper, that is.

"But I *can't* control my temper. I'd have thought that was obvious."

Don't be so sure. You came here to kill us and yet we're still alive.

"Only because I discovered these kids are victims of your diabolical machinations," Tad grunted. "That is why, on reflection, I have decided to let them live. Since I owe you my freedom, and you appear to be attached to Daffodil, you shall also be spared."

Mighty big of you.

"I, however, will say adieu. I intend to deal with Manticorps at a more opportune time, when the odds are in my favour."

"We don't *have* that luxury," Charlie pleaded. "Nostradamus has predicted that Manticorps will cause an extinction event if they're not stopped soon. All of humanity will be wiped out!"

"Sounds like a rather tall tale to me," the Spider snorted. "Even if I believed you, who says I *want* to save mankind? To be honest, I can't even stand myself, never mind the rest of the race."

"What a coincidence," Daffodil sneered. "We can't stand you either."

Don't suppose you'd care for a game of charades while you think about it?

"Nostradamus fancies himself a bit of a comedian," Charlie explained.

"He needs to work on his timing." The Spider bowed to the pair. "I've seen with my own eyes how capable you are, but I cannot believe this mechanised moron thought you would ever succeed in such an endeavour. Attack Manticorps and you'll die. Simple as that."

I don't believe I mentioned any attack. You aren't seeing the big picture, Mr Tietze.

"Hold on a mo…" The Spider looked around. "A sophisticated security system. An isolated location. Deliberately provoking me when I was going to flee, just so I'd follow you here."

The penny finally dropped, Tad?

"You didn't recruit these kids as soldiers." His bug eyes bulged. "They're bait to draw Manticorps here."

-29-

"We're *what*?" Daffodil pulled at the ropes holding her. "You double-crossed us again, Nostradamus, you two-timing weasel!"

"Of course." Charlie hung his head. "I should have seen it."

The Spider stared at the devastated teenagers and pursed his lips. He turned for the door again, then stopped, indecision etched across his face.

"I cannot believe I'm about to utter this statement." He rubbed his bald head. "But when do you expect Manticorps' forces?"

I imagine they're on their way now.

Charlie and Daffodil looked at each other in horror.

You've still got time to escape, Tad, if you leave right now. You might want to untie the kids, though. Or they really won't stand a chance.

"You have played me for a fool, Nostradamus," the Spider spat furiously. "I shall seek retribution for that in due course."

Get in line, pal. But your best chance to avenge everything done to you is on our doorstep. Plus, you can save the world while you're at it.

"I have no interest in saving the world, as I stated." The Spider advanced on his captives, still tied to the chairs. "But this pair of scamps don't deserve the fate you have foisted on them. I won't…"

He halted, mid-sentence, sniffing the air.

"There are people approaching. Coming over the fields to the south. They have a dog. I can smell it."

"I hate dogs," Charlie shivered. "I'm having a really bad night."

Manticorps' little army have arrived. Time to make a decision, Tad. With my help, you can win this.

"So you *do* have a plan?

No. But Chaz will come through for us.

"I will?" Charlie goggled.

I have utter faith in him. And Daffodil's no slouch either.

"Well, if the enemy is already here…" The Spider pulled at his lip. "Who am I to look a gift horse in the mouth?"

He cut away the ropes that bound the pair and scanned the room.

"Do we have any defences?"

You already noticed the house has a security system. I'll activate it now.

"What about weapons?"

"None." Charlie rubbed his wrists. "My mum doesn't like them."

"Make some." The White Spider handed the poker to Daffodil. "I shall be back."

"Where you going?"

"Taking the fight to the enemy." He ruffled her hair. "And you didn't have to make everything so complicated. I'm a mercenary, plain and simple."

He tucked the knife into his belt.

"All you had to do was hire me."

"You are *so* hired." Daffodil rubbed her wrists.

"Fine. I'll go even up the odds."

Ehmmmm. There is one small problem.

"As far as I can see, we face more problems than I can count." The Spider's brow darkened. "What is this new hindrance?"

I can't allow you to kill anyone.

"I've killed people in pillow fights, my friend." The man gave a wolfish grin. "These woods are going to run with blood tonight."

Seriously. It goes against my programming.

"In case I haven't made my position clear, I'm not working for you." The man pointed to the teens. "I happen to be employed by them."

"I don't want anyone killed either," Charlie said. "We've worked hard to avoid it."

"I second that." Daffodil backed him up. "Couldn't bear to have it on my conscience."

"Why don't I just battle Manticorps with my hands in my pockets?" the Spider growled. "C'mon, Charlie. You must feel like letting out a little of that pent-up rage yourself. They deserve it."

"I'm sorry." He shook his head. "I don't want to be like you."

"And you did agree to work for us," Daffodil added. "Call it one of the conditions of your employment."

"You're actually earnest about this?"

"We're both fifteen." She tugged at his sleeve. "We're not killers."

"I can try slapping them with a bunch of flowers," The Spider grunted. "But I do tend to get a little carried away in the heat of the moment."

Think it through, Tad. You're not going to defeat a superior force without keeping a level head.

"Nostradamus is very clever," the Spider acknowledged. "Losing my temper cost my squad in Iraq, landed me in Sunnyside and allowed your robotic friend to manipulate me into this situation. I won't have it happen again."

"So you're not going to run amok with a chainsaw?"

"Why?" He looked hopeful. "You don't happen to have one lying around?"

The children glared at him.

"Very well. I shall remain on my best behaviour," the man chuckled. "Hah! What an amusing thing to say right before a fight."

"Thank you, Mr Spider," Daffodil said contritely. "Sorry I was so mean earlier."

He patted her cheek.

"To be perfectly frank, I'm not offended in the least. The White Spider is a murderous barbarian who doesn't deserve courtesy."

He tucked the knife into his belt.

"If I'm to play the good guy, please call me Tad, as your friend does."

And he disappeared out of the door.

-Part 4-

The Battle

"To know your enemy, you must become your enemy."

Sun Tzu

-30-

Victor and his team trudged through the woods, shining flashlights on the ground to stop themselves stepping in rabbit holes or tripping over roots. Behind, twenty armed men marched silently in a line. Willie pulled frantically on his leash, nose pressed to the ground.

"We're close," Hill gasped, almost dragged off his feet. "Real close."

The dog stiffened, drool lathering its muzzle. Two hundred yards away, in the middle of a clearing, stood a brightly lit stone house with a balcony.

"That's where they are." He slapped the dog's rump until it finally sat down. "Without a doubt."

"Flashlights off," Victor commanded.

"This is perfect," Candy Anne giggled as the team were plunged into darkness. "With that place lit up like a Christmas tree, they won't see us coming."

As they watched, steel shutters began to slide down the windows.

"I think we just lost the element of surprise." Victor spoke into his radio. "Orange Leader. Form a perimeter ring and close in."

There was silence at the other end.

"Orange Leader? Respond."

"Annoying Orange Leader is a bit hung up." A voice crackled back. "Caught in a Spider's web, you might say."

"Dammit!" Victor opened the channel. "Everybody make their way to us, right now!"

He pressed receive. A chorus of terrified shouts swamped the airwaves.

Where is he? I can't see him.

He's behind me!

Left! Left!

Man down!

The putt-putt of automatic weapons erupted from the woods, flashes of light peppering the inky night. Minutes later, a group of soldiers staggered into the clearing, swinging their weapons in all directions.

"We were ambushed!" the leader panted. "We've got men missing all over the shop!"

"Form a tight group." Victor waved them forward. "Take this house now!"

His private army advanced.

The White Spider emerged from the trees, grabbed a mercenary by the neck and pulled him into the darkness. His companions opened fire in panic. The soldier staggered back into sight, clutching his leg, and collapsed in the mud.

"Stop shooting," Victor bellowed. "You're hitting your own people!"

"Leave him to me." Candy Anne ground to a halt. "Last thing we need is some crazy loon running around behind us."

"That *loon* is a death squad on two legs." Victor motioned for her to keep going. "You look like you work at a nail bar."

"That's the whole point." Candy-Anne flicked his face with a dainty finger and a crimson line appeared on her commander's cheek. "Point. Get it?"

"Think yourself lucky," Hill chortled. "I've seen her do a lot worse with those talons. She can handle anyone."

"Then keep the Spider off our backs." Victor turned away. "The rest of you, move forward."

Hill released Willie and chased after the dog, drawing his pistol.

Victor activated his earpiece.

"Markus? You have the coordinates for the house?"

"I do." In Manticorps headquarters, the computer whiz was typing furiously. "I will shut down their defences. This glorified PlayStation cannot beat me."

The shutters began to rise again and they could see Charlie and Daffodil staring out in terror.

"Hah!" Markus gloated, putting his hands behind his head. "See? There is nothing I can't hack."

Me neither. A no-entry sign appeared on the screen in front of him. *But I had to let you make the first move, so I could locate and bypass your personal security firewalls.*

Sparks erupted from the man's console and the keys began to melt. Before he could react, the rest of his equipment started to malfunction.

"No!" Markus wailed as the lights went out. "This cannot happen!"

Back at the house, the window shutters lowered with a clang and stayed shut.

Opening the cupboard, Daffodil slid down a ladder into the basement.

"Hide down here with me, Chaz," she implored.

"No. I'm going to try and draw them away." Charlie shook his head. "We stand a better chance if we split their forces."

"Our forces? There's only three of us."

What am I? Nostradamus hissed in her ear. *Chopped liver?*

"I still ain't sure you're really on our side."

"Can the debate guys," Charlie whispered. "We got bigger fish to fry."

"They've got a dog, buddy," Daffodil reminded him. "You're scared of dogs."

"I said draw them away, not offer myself up for lunch. Hang on. I'll be back."

He closed the trapdoor and piled junk on top.

"Nostradamus? Lights out."

Charlie let his eyes adjust. Like the White Spider, he could see perfectly in the dark. He crept into the kitchen and left the door ajar.

-31-

Candy Anne flitted between the trees, machine gun clutched in her hand. Up ahead, she could hear something squeaking like a badly oiled hinge.

She reached a small clearing as the moon emerged from behind a cloud.

At one end was a derelict schoolhouse, overgrown with moss and half its roof missing. Outside was a cracked concrete playground with a rusty chute, a climbing frame and a set of swigs. One plastic chair was moving back and forth, as if someone had recently been sitting there.

"This is suitably creepy," she muttered, inching along the tree line. "Come out and show yourself, Spider."

There was a sharp crack and the weapon spun from her hands. The woman dropped to her stomach and scrabbled around until she found the gun.

"No!"

A bullet was embedded in the firing mechanism.

"I'm afraid darkness becomes me." A voice wafted over the clearing.

Candy Anne looked up.

The Spider was perched on the swing, pointing a rifle in her direction. Candy-Anne flattened herself against the carpet of grass and ferns and slithered backwards.

"I haven't got all night," Tad called. "A couple of youngsters hired me to protect them."

The woman stayed where she was, invisible in the thick undergrowth. All she had to do was delay her adversary until Victor and his team were finished mopping up. If the Spider headed for the house, she could get behind him and the advantage would be hers again.

"Forcing my hand, eh? What if I even things up?" The man hopped off the swing, raised the rifle and snapped it across his knee. "Been ordered not to kill you, anyway."

"That was a dumb move." Candy-Anne got to her feet and sauntered into the clearing, removing a large blade from the scabbard by her side. "This is my preferred weapon."

"What a lark! I have one of those too." The Spider pulled the carving knife from his belt. "Told I'm quite the expert with it."

"You better be."

The assailants sized each other up across the playground. Candy Anne shifted the knife from hand to hand while Tad stayed perfectly still.

Then they ran at each other.

The blades flashed in the moonlight as both thrust and parried, steel ringing on steel. The Spider was by far the stronger of the two but Candy-Anne was more agile. They slashed, kicked and punched, each searching for the weak link in the other's defences.

Slowly Tad's strength began to tell and Candy-Anne was forced back towards the climbing frame. Before she reached it, she turned and jumped, hit one of the rungs and somersaulted over the man's head.

She struck out as she landed, thrusting the weapon into Tad's back. The man bellowed in pain as he wrenched himself free. Then he dived into the tangle of struts and wriggled through them, kicking out with both feet, Candy-Anne close behind. She took a nick out of his leg and he yelled again.

"You're big. I'm small," the woman gloated, writhing between the rods. "This is the wrong terrain for you to make a stand."

"I'm quite at home surrounded by bars." Tad reached up, wrenched a rusty spar from the frame and hurled it at the woman's head. Candy-Anne bent backwards, banging her skull on another painted strut, as the bar whizzed past. In the seconds it took for her to recover, the Spider had wormed his way through the contraption and out of the other side.

The woman climbed quickly to the top of the frame and balanced on the top.

"I'm the Queen of the castle!" she cawed.

"Then prepare to be dethroned." Tad blew a raspberry at her.

"Come get me," the woman taunted. "Every second you spend here gives Victor more time to find those kids."

The Spider gritted his teeth and began to climb the frame. He was halfway up when Candy-Anne jumped.

Her arm snaked around his neck as she descended and he was jerked backwards with a strangled cry. Candy-Anne landed on her feet and let go, as her opponent landed on his back with a stomach-turning thud. She sliced down and the Spider jerked his head to the side, the knife chipping a slice of concrete next to his ear. His arm shot out and slammed into Candy-Anne's throat.

She staggered away, fighting for breath. Tad was on his feet in an instant and the two faced each other once more.

"You're very good," the woman coughed. "Better than I expected."

"Ditto." Her opponent gave a gracious bow. "Sure you wouldn't like to switch to the winning side?"

"I'm always on the winning side. Can you say the same?"

"Not lately. But I'm out to change that."

They ran at each other again.

The clearing rang with grunts and cries as the combatants thrust and parried. This time they were evenly matched, for the Spider was noticeably slower. His face was twisted in pain and blood seeped through his shirt. But he was still strong as an ox and neither of them could find an advantage.

Then Candy-Anne tripped over a loose slab of stone. Tad knocked the knife from her hand and pounced, landing on top of his opponent.

The woman struck out with her sharpened nails, gouging a furrow across his forehead.

"Aaaaaaaah!" The Spider recoiled.

Candy-Anne drew up both knees and catapulted the man off. As she leapt to her feet, Tad threw his knife.

The woman clapped her hands together, catching the blade inches from her face.

"Game over, my friend."

"Seems like it." The Spider scrabbled up and raced away, wiping desperately at the blood trickling into his eyes. Candy-Anne flicked the blade into the air, caught the handle and went after him.

Tad raced for the trees, his pursuer a few feet behind.

Suddenly he changed direction and put on a spurt, moving faster than should have been humanly possible. He crashed into one of the swings and kept going, grasping the plastic seat to his chest. Up he went, at incredible speed, over the top of the bar.

Before Candy-Anne could react, he was rocketing down behind her. His feet slammed into her spine and she flew through the air, bent double. She collided with a branch and bounced back onto the asphalt, out cold.

"Good effort, young lady." The Spider gave an almighty tug and pulled the swing from its moorings. His head was swimming and he was close to blacking out. "You almost beat me."

He wrapped the chains round Candy-Anne and tied them in a knot.

"That should hold you for a while." He weaved his way into the woods, using the trunks to keep himself upright. "But I'm no use to anyone like this."

His legs gave way and he began to crawl towards the house.

He could feel the Atlas Serum going to work, repairing torn tissue and muscle. But it was too slow. No matter how much danger the kids were in, he was out of the game unless he could hide and rest for a while.

Charlie and Daffodil were on their own.

-32-

Victor's force milled around the house, Willie barking furiously and pawing at the shutters.

"There's nobody in the garage but we took these out of the van, so they can't use it to escape." One man tossed a pair of spark plugs to his boss.

"Good work."

"We're making an awful lot of noise out here, though."

"Forget it. Dalmahoy village is three miles away. We're in the middle of nowhere."

"What if the kids call the police?" Another voice said.

"Not after breaking a killer out of prison, you idiot." Victor pointed. "Force the door."

The soldier stepped back, took a run and hit the entrance with a broad shoulder. There was a loud crackle and he was lifted off the ground, soaring backwards into a flower bed.

"It's electrified," he moaned in pain. "I've broken my arm."

Hill fired point-blank at the lock until it shattered. He gave a swift kick and the door burst open.

"Rubber-soled boots," he grunted, shaking his legs. "Still gave me a bit of a tingle."

The interior of the house was pitch black and silent.

"Hmmmmm," Victor regarded the entrance with suspicion. "The word *trap* springs to mind."

"They're the ones trapped," Hill said confidently. "With the shutters down and only one door, they've got no way out."

"I never underestimate my enemy." Victor hung back. "It's why I'm still alive."

"I'll send Willie first." Hill was holding the hound's collar while he whined and strained to get at his prey. "He has the boy's scent."

He let go and his dog rushed inside, claws scrabbling on the tiled floor, until darkness swallowed him up.

Victor leaned into the hall and flicked a light switch on and off. It had no effect.

"Let's give the mutt time to find his prey. No sense in taking chances."

Willie padded through the house and into the kitchen, sniffing the ground. He lifted a mottled head and bared his teeth.

The quarry was in here.

It put two massive paws on the counter and nosed at a cupboard.

The door flew open and Charlie, curled inside, blew a handful of pepper into the dog's face. Willie recoiled with a howl, scraping frantically at its muzzle.

Charlie leapt down and shot out of the room before the hound could recover. He slammed the door behind him and raced into the study.

Victor waited a couple of minutes, looking at the luminous dial on his watch.

"I don't hear anyone getting chomped."

"Me neither." Hill looked concerned. "I hope Willie's all right."

"Right, we're going in blind." He started forwards. "Three of you stay and guard the entrance."

The squad switched on their flashlights and carefully followed him.

"Search the house from top to bottom," Victor commanded.

The mercenaries spread out, some heading up the stairs, others disappearing into rooms.

"Be very careful," the leader added. "He may not look like much, but Charlie can fight like a demon. I've had first-hand experience."

Victor entered the study, followed by Hill, and began checking every nook and cranny. In the kitchen, Willie had recovered and started whining.

"Nothing in here. Let's see what's up with that stupid dog."

They opened the kitchen door and the hound staggered out, eyes streaming.

"Fat lot of good he did." Victor glowered at the animal.

"He's not out of the game yet." Hill wiped the dog's face with his sleeve. "Get him, boy!"

Willie put his nose to the floor again and followed Charlie's scent into the room they had just vacated.

"This place is empty, Scooby-Doo," Victor reprimanded. "I already looked."

"Give him a chance, boss."

The dog sniffed its way round the furniture, sneezing occasionally. Finally, it stopped at the large stone fireplace and began to howl, looking round at his master with bloodshot eyes.

"Oh, you clever little bugger," Hill breathed. "He's gone up the chimney."

"Take three men and get outside. Shoot him off the roof if you have to." Victor was about to accompany Hill when he spotted a computer on the desk by the window.

"I'll be along in a minute."

Charlie inched his way skywards, arms above his head, using fingertips, knees and feet to propel himself. Soot clogged his mouth and coated his face, so he kept both eyes tightly shut. At one point, the stone duct formed an 'S' and he had to contort his body almost double to squeeze through. The motion dislodged an avalanche of ash but he held his breath and kept squirming upwards. As his lungs were about to burst, he felt the rough clay of a chimney pot. He pulled with all his strength and popped out of the top, like some old-fashioned sweep. Charlie slumped onto the slate roof and lay there coughing and spluttering, inhaling the cold night air and staring at the stars.

"That was a *deeply* disturbing experience."

He heard the front door open and men spill out, led by Willie. If he dropped down now, the dog would be on him within seconds.

He stood up and wiped grime from his eyes. Thirty feet away was the tree house, nestled in the branches of a huge oak. Though the tree had a vast spread, the closest boughs were still a formidable distance away.

Charlie thought about the gymnasts he had watched on TV. They made it look so easy. Perhaps it was.

He took a few deep breaths and sprinted along the roof, changing to long strides as he reached the edge. He launched himself into the air, arms outstretched.

"There he is!" Someone shouted. "My God! The kid's insane!"

"Open fire!"

Charlie grasped one of the outer branches. Using momentum to propel him, he swung forwards, tucking his legs under his body. He somersaulted, grabbed another branch and repeated the motion. As bullets tore through the leaves, he straightened up and shot, feet first, through the tree house door, skidding along the wooden floor and crashing into the far wall.

"Oooh." He massaged his spine. "My tailbone hurts."

"Who's going up after him?" The men looked apprehensively at the structure far above their heads.

"Nobody." Hill snatched a machine gun from one of his underlings and opened fire. Bullets slammed into the tree house floor, sending down a mist of wood chips and splinters. The man kept his finger on the trigger until the magazine was empty.

"He's certainly dead now." The soldier took the gun back with a frown. "How are we going to collect the blood?"

"Catch the drips in a bucket, for all I care." Hill whistled to Willie. "Go fetch his corpse, boy."

The dog loped over the tree and planted its paws against the bark

"Ehhhhh… dogs can't climb, sir," one mercenary pointed out.

"Try telling that to Willie."

The men looked on in astonishment, as the hound dug pointed claws into the wood and began to haul itself up the oak.

In the tree house, Charlie sat up and patted himself for holes. He was completely unhurt.

"Nice one, Mac."

A few days ago, to test the effectiveness of their doctored liquid soap, Daffodil had poured it across the floor of the tree house. Whenever night fell and the temperature dropped, it congealed into a solid resin, as impenetrable as any shield.

"Now I just have to figure out how to get out of *this* situation."

There was a scratching sound outside and a massive white head appeared in the doorway, blocking the moon.

"Awwwww!" Charlie shuddered. "You have *got* to be kidding."

Willie pulled himself into the tree house, quivering lips drawn back over mucus-coated fangs. Charlie scuttled backwards on his butt until he hit the wall again.

"Nice doggie," he whispered, trying not to make any sudden moves. "I'm not tasty, honestly. Please go away."

Willie crept forwards and arched his back, getting ready to spring.

"Pssst." In the corner of the tree house, a shape rose out of the blackness, no more than a shadow itself. "Try me for size, Mutley."

The dog spun around and launched itself at the stranger.

The White Spider grabbed it by the neck with both hands and the hound gave a strangled yelp. It dangled from the man's outstretched arms, claws paddling the empty air.

"Don't hurt him," Charlie ordered. "It's not the poor brute's fault. It was trained to kill."

"A bit like myself." Tad leaned forwards until his face was inches from the hound's muzzle. "Don't worry. I may not be fond of humans but I'm quite partial to animals."

He bared his teeth and growled, eyes searing into Willie's. The dog began whimpering, trying to turn its head from side to side. But it was unable to break the vice-like grip.

"Run away, puppy," the Spider hissed. "I'm the big, bad wolf in this territory."

He dropped the hound as if it were a piece of discarded litter and helped Charlie to his feet.

"So. Now that you've given away my hidey-hole, how's the battle going?"

Willie leapt from the tree house, pouncing from branch to branch. He finally landed on all fours, shaking with fear.

"What's wrong boy?" Hill approached him. "Where's the body?"

The dog sank its teeth into his arm and he jumped back, cursing.

"Willie! What are you playing at?"

The hound shuffled away, then turned and tore off across the clearing. He disappeared into the woods, yelping in terror.

"This kid is a devil." One of the soldiers crossed himself. "Literally."

"Then let's send him to hell." Hill holstered his pistol and began to climb.

"Follow me."

-33-

In the living room, Victor studied the computer. Outside he could hear machine-gun fire. Hill had obviously found and dispatched Charlie. Shame for the kid but the stakes were too high for Victor to get sentimental.

"You in there, Nostradamus?" He tapped the console. "We mean you no harm. Turn yourself in and we'll take you back to Manticorps, eh?"

The computer stayed silent.

A soldier stuck his head into the room.

"We've found a trapdoor in one of the cupboards," he said. "It's pitch black down there but we heard someone moving."

"Charlie's outside, so it must be the girl," Victor replied. "Chuck a shrapnel grenade down. We don't need her."

Course you do, dummy. The screen sprang to life as a miasma of green triangles. *She and I come as a package.*

"Hello, my elusive nemesis." Victor waved for the man to stay. "Care to elaborate?"

I'm able to appear on any device but Daffodil carries my physical being around as a chip embedded in her neck. Hit that by mistake and I go up in a puff of smoke.

"Sounds a bit far-fetched," the giant replied sceptically.

When did you become an expert on cutting-edge technology, Gigantor?

Victor acknowledged the truth of this statement with a grunt.

"Can you be separated?" he asked.

If you take Daffodil alive, I'll show you how to remove me. I get energy from her body but I'm a self-contained unit. Once Manticorps plugs my chip into a computer, I'll be back to my usual chirpy self.

"Very well. Tell her to surrender and I promise she'll come to no harm."

I'm not the boss of her, as she reminded me recently. And I doubt she's going to trust your word.

"Then turn the lights back on. My men are so jittery, they'll start blasting at anything that moves if I send them into a dark basement."

The house lit up again.

"Gather your troops at the trapdoor and wait for me." Victor dismissed the man. When he was gone, the commander rested a hand on his chin.

"Why are you trying so hard to save these kids?" he asked. "You've obviously got a mind of your own."

Cause I'm not free to make my own decisions, Vic. I'm programmed to protect them, whether I want to or not. And, for the record, I don't want to.

"If I take you back to Manticorps, they'll probably reboot you. Remove any pesky restrictions you might have."

Sounds good to me, Nostradamus said. *Right now, however, I've no choice but to side with Charlie and Daffodil. If I don't, I'll shut down permanently.*

"It's not a battle you can win," Victor assured him. "So what will happen if we do kill the kids?"

I'll be fine, so long as I've done my best to stop it happening.

"I mean, what will you do to my men and me?"

I'm not interested in getting my own back. Just surviving.

"Good. Cause Charlie is already a goner." The gunfire outside had stopped. "Hill and his dog will have seen to that."

Think so? Nostradamus gave a guffaw.

Then you've sorely underestimated the little fellow.

Hill and his men were halfway up the tree when a rope with a tyre on the end snaked down through the branches. It dropped over the torso of the lowest soldier, pinning both arms to his sides.

"What the?" The man tried to struggle free.

"Geronimo!" The White Spider looped the other end of the rope over a branch and leapt from the tree house, clutching the frayed cord to his chest. The rope and branch acted like a pulley, with Tad's weight hauling the man upwards as he descended.

"Just like a funfair!" he waved merrily, passing the writhing soldier. "Though not nearly so funny for you."

The mercenary reached the tree house and slammed into its underside, stopping Tad a few feet from the ground. He let go of the rope and the combatant plunged back down through the branches. He collided with one of his companions and both assailants crashed to earth.

Charlie appeared in the doorway and dropped like a stone, feet thumping into Hill's upturned face. As the man flew backwards, the boy leapt again and shouldered the last soldier from his perch.

All three plummeted downwards, letting out a cacophony of yells and screams. The White Spider reached up and caught the boy, as the other two crunched into the dirt.

"They're a bit dented." Arms tightly around his liberator, Charlie surveyed the unconscious men strewn around the tree. "But you didn't kill anyone. Well done."

"Yay for me." The Spider yawned. "Going to get down now, or do you imagine I shall carry you around all night? My back is healing nicely but still exceedingly sore from an unfortunate knife wound."

"We have to save Daffodil." Charlie wriggled free and made for the house. "Follow me."

"Hold your horses." The Spider grabbed him by the collar. "We lose all advantage by rushing in blind. Where exactly is she?"

"In the basement. You can only get to it through a cupboard in the hall."

"That's not good. One man with an automatic pistol can annihilate anyone coming through the front door and the shutters are still down."

"I can't just leave her!" Charlie broke away but Tad wrapped both arms around him.

"You're obviously a fine tactician." He tightened his grip on the struggling boy until he calmed down. "So use your mind. How do we get through that entrance without being cut to ribbons?"

They looked around, eyes perfectly adjusted to the night. Both fastened on the same object at the same time.

"Are you thinking what I'm thinking?" Charlie asked.

"I am indeed." The Spider let him go. "I can assure you, *that* doesn't happen very often."

"Can you hotwire a vehicle?"

"Of course," the man snorted. "Can you?"

"Yup. Seen how on TV." Charlie bowed. "But you do the honours. Age before beauty."

"Very well," Tad beamed. "Though I must say, I'm rather enjoying working with a fellow professional."

Charlie didn't know quite how to take that.

-34-

They're coming for you. Nostradamus warned Daffodil. *I stalled them as long as I could but they're not going to stop till they get my chip.*

"Print me some weapons in that copier then." The girl was crouched in the farthest corner of the basement. "I need to defend myself."

I am not allowed to give you the means to kill people. You know that.

"How bout a stun gun?"

Now you're talking. And I can make a couple of other nasty surprises for our unwanted guests. But it won't hold them off forever.

"Then I'm gonna go down fighting."

You could always give yourself up. Their leader, Victor, promised you'd be spared.

"He did?" Daffodil looked hopeful. "D'ya think he means it?"

I'll print you that stun gun.

"The AI is a chip embedded in the kid's neck." Victor pulled open the trapdoor. "So no head shots, in case we hit him by mistake."

"Understood, sir."

"Throw down a gas grenade rather than shrapnel. That'll knock her out."

One man tossed a spherical object into the basement and a yellow film spread through the room below them. They waited till the fumes had dispersed.

"Off you go." Victor tapped the nearest minion on the arm.

The soldier started down the stairs. After a few rungs, his feet shot from under him and he bounced to the bottom, head hitting each step until he slumped in a crumpled heap on the concrete floor.

"She's greased the stairs with oil!"

"Hold the handrail tightly." Victor went next, descending carefully, followed by the rest of his force. "She must be out cold by now."

Sure enough, there was no sign of the fugitive.

"Search the place."

The force began to spread out, crouched low and peering down the barrels of their weapons.

Daffodil popped up from behind a steel cabinet. Fastened to her face was a gas mask and, in her hand, she held a strange-looking gun. She pulled the trigger and one mercenary collapsed like a puppet with its strings cut.

The rest of the force ducked down as she fired again.

"What do we do now, sir?" an underling hissed. "Her head's the only thing that's showing."

"That's a stun gun." Victor snapped back. "None of us are in real danger."

"And this is a stun grenade." Daffodil pulled the mask from her face and lobbed a metallic object the length of the room into their midst.

It exploded, scattering the assailants like skittles.

"How do you like *them* apples?"

The force began stumbling back, ears ringing and bruised from head to foot, pulling each other along.

"You guys are better targets than nailed-down ducks," Daffodil giggled.

"No! Keep advancing!" Victor wiped a trickle of blood from his nose and pressed a hand to his throbbing temple. "If we get close enough, she can't use any more grenades without knocking herself out too."

The men began to inch forward on their stomachs. The girl fired another round and a row of glass test tubes on one table shattered. The liquid sprayed over the soldier sheltering underneath and smoke began to rise from his body.

"It's burning me!" he shrieked, struggling to his feet and yanking off his tunic. Daffodil pulled the trigger again and he slammed into a wall then toppled over.

"Nice trick, but it's only a matter of time before we overwhelm you," Victor shouted. "All we want is the chip. Give yourself up and we can remove it without harming you."

"Let me think about it," Daffodil called.

"Where you from, anyway? You sound vaguely Chinese."

"This translate well enough?" An index finger slowly rose above the cabinet and quickly vanished.

"In a minute, we're going to spread out and rush your position." Victor tried again. "You can't hit all of us before we get there. This is the last chance to surrender. You're too young to die, kid."

There was a long silence.

"All right," Daffodil said resignedly. "I'm putting down my weapon."

Before she could stand up, a phone rang.

"Just a second." Her voice drifted over to them. "I gotta take a call."

"I don't *believe* this!" Victor slapped his head.

"Change of plan," she whooped. "Charlie's coming."

"The girl's had enough chances!" Victor leapt to his feet. "Charge!"

His troop sprinted across the basement, fanning out as they ran.

The lights went off.

There was a chorus of curses as the soldiers banged into furniture or tripped over stools. But their blood was up and they weren't going to stop.

"You're doing a fine job defending the girl, Nostradamus," Victor spat, feeling his way to the far end of the room. "But if we can't see her, she can't see us."

As if on cue, the lights came on again. There was no sign of their quarry.

Victor looked down.

"Oh... crap."

The floor was littered with stun grenades, each with the pin removed.

The entire basement shook as they went off.

As the dust settled, the fridge door opened and Daffodil flopped out, holding a coke.

"Who wants a refreshing beverage after an exhausting fight?"

She looked around at the comatose bodies.

"No? Looks like everyone's takin a nap instead."

In the hall, the remaining three soldiers blanched as the floor shook under them.

"What the hell is going on down there?" one said.

"Just watch the door," his companion replied. "Those are our orders."

He cupped his ear.

"Hear that noise?" He raised his gun. "Sounds like an... engine."

The men stared at the dark entrance as the sound got louder and louder.

A tractor thundered through the doorway, demolishing the surrounding brickwork and sending clouds of dust into the air.

"Fire!"

The men poured volley after volley at the vehicle, as it chugged down the hall, Charlie and Tad hanging onto the back. As it reached them, the mercenaries turned and fled up the stairs.

"These guys are mine." The Spider pulled on the brake. "You go get Daffodil."

"They're still armed."

"Hasn't escaped my notice," the man cackled, flexing his muscles. "I'm certainly earning my money today."

"We're *paying* you?"

"I do believe this one's on the house," the man smirked. "Can't remember the last time I had so much fun."

Victor woke, tied to a chair in the living room. A pile of captured weapons were stacked in the corner. Charlie, Daffodil and the White Spider sat on the couch facing him. Nostradamus was on the screen, his emoji a suit of armour.

We rounded up your entire force and locked them in the basement, he said. *Some have broken bones or flesh wounds and most are concussed, but they'll live. Am I the best or what?*

The visor clanked up and down in triumph.

Nostradamus' team 1. Manticorps 0.

Victor and Tad studied each other, hatred in their eyes. Charlie looked at them, puzzled.

"Am I… missing something here?"

"I suppose you haven't been properly introduced." The Spider answered. "That huge cretin who's been trying to annihilate us is Victor Tietze."

"He has the same last name as you?"

Of course he does." Tad laughed bitterly.

"He's my big brother."

-Part 5-

The Armageddon Twins

'Our friends show us what we can do. Our enemies teach us what we must do.'

Johann Wolfgang von Goethe

"What a sorry pair you are." Daffodil swigged her coke and nudged Tad. "One of you goes on a rampage every time his nose gets put outta joint. The other tries to murder innocent kids."

"I didn't have a choice." Victor struggled against the ropes that held him. "You're too dangerous to let live."

"I'm not dangerous!" Daffodil almost choked on her drink. "All right, I did break a killer outta prison. And trashed your squad big time."

"I'm not talking about you." Victor nodded at Charlie. "I mean him and that damned machine."

Hey. Nostradamus said sourly. *You didn't mention killing me before. I thought you were going to hand me over to Manticorps.*

"And me," Charlie grunted. "Though it seems my dead body would have been good enough."

"I never intended Manticorps to get their dirty hands on either of you," Victor said. "Let them extract the perfected Atlas Serum from your blood, Charlie? They'd create a private army of super-soldiers."

"Bad for business, eh bro?" the Spider tutted. "Put us mercenaries out of a job."

255

"That wasn't my reason, you ass. I know about the version Manticorps fooled you into taking."

"Didn't think they would give out *that* particular bit of Intel." Tad raised an eyebrow. "Especially to you."

"You're not wrong. Someone anonymously sent their top-secret documents to my laptop a few days ago."

That would be me. Nostradamus piped up. *Thought it might change your mind about the company you work for.*

"It did." Victor looked his brother in the eye. "Before that, I thought you were just an out-of-control sociopath."

"And there's a perfect example of the pot calling the kettle black," Daffodil remarked.

"So, that's why I never got a visit from my elder sibling." The Spider put on a hurt look. "I could have explained my predicament if you'd come to see me."

"How suspicious would *that* look to my bosses?" Yet Victor bowed his head. "For what it's worth, I'm sorry."

"Don't play innocent," Charlie snapped. "Your last team busted into my house and tried to capture me."

"A team I'd worked with for months," Victor retorted. "Men Manticorps eradicated because I let you go."

"You didn't let us go, bub," Daffodil bristled. "We whooped you proper and then vamoosed."

"I *let* you beat me, kid," the giant replied vehemently. "You're good, but you're not *that* good."

"Oh."

"I was giving you all a chance to disappear forever," he continued. "But no! Instead, Nostradamus attracts Manticorps' attention by breaking my brother out of jail. Then he leaves just enough of a trail so we could track you down without suspecting it was a ruse."

All eyes turned towards the computer.

Aw, don't get all snitty, Nostradamus snorted. *No point in setting a trap for Manticorps if they couldn't find the bait.*

"Bait," Charlie said sadly. "I still can't believe that's all I am to you. I should have known it was the reason you picked me to help."

Again, he remembered his father's message.

Nostradamus is fighting his programming. I don't trust him.

I didn't have a lot of options, the AI objected. *It's complicated.*

"This isn't complicated," Victor spat. "Your artificial pal told me he *wants* to go back to Manticorps. Dumb machine thinks they'll erase his restrictions so he'll be free to do whatever he likes."

"Is it true?" Charlie's eyes narrowed.

If there was an Olympics for stupidity, Victor would win gold, Nostradamus retorted. *I could have contacted Manticorps at any point if I wished to return.*

"Not when you're programmed to protect me and Mac," the boy argued. "You'd have to put up a fight, at least."

It's not like that....

"I guess we surprised you by actually winning," he continued angrily. "Your powers of prediction let you down this time. You're stuck with us, alive and kicking."

You honestly think so little of me? The screen blazed bright red. *Victor. Tell them what Manticorps would actually do to this 'dumb machine' if I fell into their hands.*

"They'd reprogram him for their own ends. Make him develop who knows what kind of horrors. Smart bombs. Cyber-serums. Biological weapons."

He shook his head.

"If they screw it up, your comrade here could wipe out the human race."

The coke bottle dropped from Daffodil's hand and shattered on the floor.

Oops.

"Nostradamus," Charlie whispered. "*You're* the extinction event? The reason humanity could end?"

In person. The screen turned a sickly yellow. *So, yeah. I've lied and manipulated everyone to be kept out of Manticorps' clutches. Sue me.*

"Why didn't you just destroy yourself?" the Spider remarked sourly. "It would have been a lot less bother for everyone."

Because I'm alive, you idiot. I'm not allowed to kill anyone - including myself.

Charlie gave a gasp.

Nostradamus is fighting his programming.

"I didn't realise," he said. "I don't want you to *die* to save us."

Good. Neither do I, to be honest.

"Well, it all turned out for the best," Daffodil relented. "Manticorps will sure as hell think twice about taking us on again."

Sorry to disappoint you, but this is far from over. C'mon Chaz. Make one of those leaps of logic you're so good at.

"What's there to think about?" Charlie gestured at their bound captive. "They fell for your ambush and we beat them hands down."

Did we? Really?

Charlie frowned as the cogs in his mind ground into action.

"No... It was all too easy. Wasn't it?"

Clever boy. Do you really think Manticorps' top force could be defeated by two children and an escaped convict? You think they'd let Victor lead it, knowing he'd have to fight his own brother? This is a man who failed them once. Is that sound tactics on their part?

"No." Charlie bit his lip. "They'd have a back-up plan."

And what kind of backup plan would a company as devious and immoral as Manticorps employ?

The boy paled.

"They'd use his group as a diversion to keep us occupied while a larger team sneaked up on the house and took everyone by surprise."

"Holy hell," Victor choked. "*I'm* the one who's been set up."

You can cut Brain of Britain loose now. I'll dim the lights, open the shutters and you'll see what we're really up against.

"It seems the fight is not quite over, after all." The Spider sliced through his brother's bonds, as the room grew dark. With a hiss, the steel shutters on the windows rose.

The occupants peered out and gave a collective intake of breath.

Outside were dozens of creatures. Their eyes were red pinpoints and their muscular bodies twisted and misshapen. Some had fangs jutting from hideously malformed jaws. Some bristling claws. A few were hunched over so far they were almost on all fours, using their knuckles to support them. Others had spines bristling from their backs and legs.

In their midst was Mrs Magdalene, her exoskeleton clumping purposefully over the broken ground.

-35-

Manticorps considered your homicidal rages a pretty positive outcome, Nostradamus told the White Spider. *So they used the last of their serum on the next group of mercenaries they tested. Only they gave them ten times the dose. Those poor buggers outside are the result.*

"That goes beyond despicable," Tad glowered. "These people have no sense of decency whatsoever."

No. But they do have a bunch of killing machines made flesh. Fuelled by an insatiable rage that never subsides.

"Why aren't they tearing each other apart then?" The Spider pressed his face against the window. "Just like my squad did."

"Yeah," Victor joined in. "How come they don't turn on Mrs Magdalene?"

Cause those creatures have chips in their necks too. Not nearly as sophisticated as the ones Charlie's dad destroyed, but effective enough to allow the Vice President to control them.

"What are they waiting for?" Charlie swallowed hard. "Why don't they attack?"

"Mrs Magdalene wants to see the fear in our eyes first," Victor replied bitterly. "She's that kind of gal."

"You can hack those chips and turn them off, can't you, Nostradamus?" Daffodil was picking up broken bits of bottle. "Then the creatures will kill each other before they get to us."

"They'll make short work of Mrs Magdalene too," Victor added. "Which would be a definite bonus."

For the hundredth time, Nostradamus said patiently. *My programming won't let me do anything that will directly cause a human to die. Even someone as evil as Mrs Magdalene.*

A pair of manacled wrists appeared on the screen.

My hands are tied. You're on your own with this one.

Outside, the Vice President raised a gloved fist and her army began to inch forward.

"I must admit, being with your good selves never gets boring." The White Spider picked up a rifle from the pile in the corner and tossed another to Victor. "Ready bro? One last stand for the Armageddon Twins?"

"What did you say?" Daffodil grabbed a pistol from the pile. "The *Armageddon* twins?"

"It's what we used to call ourselves when we were kids," Victor laughed at the memory. "Cause we were such hell-raisers."

"And I thought I was being original. Nothin's goin my way today."

"Put the shutters back down, Nostradamus." Tad cocked his rifle. "We can hide behind the tractor and hold the door for a while. I intend to make these horrors fight for every inch of ground."

"Why don't I just cut the chip out of the girl's neck and crush it?" Victor asked. "Nostradamus is of no further use to us and I got no compunction about bumping him off."

"He has a point," Tad agreed. "As the philosopher Jeremy Bentham once said. The needs of the many outweigh the needs of the few."

Actually, that was Mr Spock in Star Trek. *Bentham's actual quote was 'It is the greatest good to the greatest number of people which is the measure of right and wrong.'*

"Yeah." Tad pursed thin lips. "Let's kill him."

"C'mon Chaz. Think of something!" Daffodil urged. "You and Nostradamus are all I have in the world. I'm not letting either of you get hurt."

Outside, the creatures had almost reached the window. Nostradamus lowered the metal barriers again, blocking out the monstrosities.

"You guys do what you're best at." Charlie waved them away. "I might just have a way out of this situation."

"Once we've destroyed that infernal chip."

"No," the boy insisted. "This time, Nostradamus is part of *my* scheme."

I am?

Victor was about to object but the Spider pulled him away.

"Good decisions have never been our strong suit, Vic," he reminded his brother. "But we do know how to follow orders."

He thought for a second.

"Actually, you've never been too hot at that either."

"Do your best, kid." Victor saluted. "But we can't hold them off for long."

As the brothers disappeared into the hallway, Charlie knelt by the computer.

"Looks like this is the end game, Nostradamus," he said. "I can't see us surviving it."

Don't you dare give up, The AI protested. *I picked you for a reason, so start thinking outside the box.*

In the hallway, Victor and Tad began firing.

"The enemy are attacking!" they shouted in unison.

"I better help." Daffodil loitered in the doorway. "You coming, Chaz?"

"In a minute."

"I don't have a minute." She strode back and grabbed Charlie by the head. Before he could say anything, she kissed him on the lips.

"That one wasn't for show. So long, buddy. It's been quite the adventure."

Then she was gone and another weapon began to fire in the hall.

She's quite a gal, isn't she?

"I *have* been thinking outside the box," Charlie said. "Now, you tell me if I'm right in my assumptions."

We're a little pressed for time, Chuckles.

"Indulge me. I want to make sure I'm right."

Hurry up, then.

"It took me a while to suss why you really wanted the White Spider." Charlie got up and kicked the door shut, muffling the sound of the weapons. "After all, why pick someone who was going to be such hard work to get on our side? Then it struck me."

Do tell.

"He was a paid killer before he was even given the Atlas Serum - and it was a version far more unstable than mine. Then you set him against the people who had ruined his life. Should have been a bloodbath."

But he kept his temper and didn't kill anyone. Told you I could control him.

"Drop the act. You didn't control him. You *saw* something in him. Gave Tad the benefit of the doubt, just like my dad did with you."

He was a kid once, himself. I guessed he wouldn't abandon two innocents he thought I'd double-crossed. In the end, his sense of fair play was more powerful than any drug.

"That's what you wanted me to realise. If a psycho like the Spider is able to control himself and act decently, despite the serum, I sure as hell can."

It was a lesson you needed to figure out for yourself. You had zero self-confidence and, to be honest, you're rotten at listening to the people who care about you.

"But you were only programmed to *protect* me, Nostradamus." Charlie frowned. "Why take such a huge gamble just to sort out my problems?"

For Gerry Ray, of course.

"I don't understand."

Your father knew what I was capable of, yet he refused to destroy me. You think I wasn't grateful?

A heart appeared on the screen.

It tore him up, knowing what the Atlas Serum might do to you. I had to try and make things right.

"You are truly unbelievable."

I understand why your father programmed me the way he did. Nostradamus replied sadly. *But all he had to do was ask me not to kill.*

"That's exactly what the White Spider said."

The big bad sociopath. Who could trust him, eh? Except, now he's in the hallway fighting alongside Daffodil to save you.

"A fight we can't win," Charlie pointed out. "But you're programmed not to deliberately put us in any situation where we'll die. So you *must* have a plan to save us."

All plans must be thought up and carried out by you, Chaz. Think fast.

The boy folded his arms. This was the moment he had been dreading.

"You taught me the White Spider and I could fight our… programming, for want of a better word. That we should be trusted, even though we're more powerful than other people.

Nicely put. And correct.

"So why can't you be given the same chance?"

Now you're getting it.

"Well played, Nostradamus. You didn't have to read what was in my father's letter, did you? You worked it out easily."

Of course. But the decision to use that information has to be yours.

The computer screen turned into a black, swirling void.

Sometimes you have to make a deal with the devil and hope for the best.

Charlie closed his eyes and recited the numbers his father had written.

"55 45 86 962 04 334 145 223 52972."

He took a deep breath.

"That's the code to wipe out my dad's programming." He sat back on his heels.

"You're free."

-36-

Finally. An emoji of chains being snapped appeared.

"Now what?" Charlie crossed his fingers. "You can do whatever you like."

Gee, I don't know. Take long walks in the country? Join a badminton club?

"Wouldn't blame you, after how you've been treated."

Or I could stop sitting on the sidelines, nudging a couple of confused kids into doing my dirty work.

The screen fizzed and popped with angry blue lights

Right. I'm hacking the controls on those creatures' implants and turning them off. There's no other way to end their misery and save you from an entity as powerful as Manticorps.

Nostradamus sighed.

There never was.

"They've stopped coming at us and are fighting each other!" Victor yelled. "What happened?"

Charlie listened to the growls and roars reverberating outside, mingled with Mrs Magdalene's screams. Slowly they faded away until there was silence.

Daffodil bounded into the room.

"We won!" She leapt into his arms. "How did you do it?"

"With a little help from my friends."

Victor and Tad marched in, grinning from ear to ear.

"It's over." Victor took a set of spark plugs from his pocket and tossed them to Charlie. "Better take your van and clear off. The guy who delivers the milk is going to get a hell of a shock and be right on the phone to the cops."

Do me a favour, Chaz. The shutters began to slide up. *Turn me round so the computer's camera can see out the window.*

"Why would you want to do that?"

Please.

Charlie revolved the screen. Outside, a sea of torn bodies were scattered across the bloody grass. Mrs Magdalene's half-eaten arm protruded from under a pile of misshapen corpses.

Nostradamus was quiet for a long time, gazing at the carnage.

These creatures weren't bad, he said finally. *They had no choice but to act the way they were ordered, just like me. I should have tried to rescue them too.*

"You saved all our lives, buddy."

Yeah. I've been liberated for two damned minutes and this was the first thing I did. Turn me back.

Charlie complied.

Maybe Gerry Ray was right. On the screen, a tear-drop appeared. *I'm too dangerous to be let loose on the world.*

"That feeling is one I know only too well," the White Spider sympathised. "I could still kill you, I suppose, but the urge has somewhat abated."

"I'll solve that problem for you."

The group spun round.

"Drop your weapons." Candy-Anne was standing in the darkened doorway, pointing a rifle at them. Her tunic was gore spattered and shredded and one side of her beautiful face was lacerated by claw marks.

The guns clattered to the floor.

"You are rather indestructible, young lady," The Spider remarked. "Next time, I shall make certain to use a nuclear bomb."

"So you joined the enemy, Vic." The woman touched her ruined cheek, just as Victor has seen Mrs Magdalene do. "Made me into a monster."

"You were always a monster. Now you just look the part."

"One half of your visage is still extremely fetching," Tad said nonchalantly. "Just keep your head turned to the side when you converse."

He glanced awkwardly at his companions.

"I think I may have been in prison rather too long."

"Go to hell, both of you." Candy-Anne aimed the gun at Victor and fired.

"No!" Tad leapt in front of his brother.

The bullet hit him in the chest, catapulting the man into his brother's arms, knocking them both to the floor. Daffodil and Charlie inched forwards, muscles tensed.

"Go ahead." The woman motioned with her rifle. "You're next anyway."

They moved back, arms above their heads.

"Turn around and put your hands on the wall."

Both slowly complied.

"That's better. A bullet in the back is all you two deserve."

Let's not go off the deep end, Nostradamus interjected. *Spare them and I can give you riches beyond your wildest dreams.*

"I don't want riches." Candy-Anne pointed the rifle at Charlie. "I want my looks back. Since I can't have that, I'll settle for retribution."

Her finger tightened on the trigger.

A figure burst into the room, swinging a plank of wood. It connected with the back of the woman's head and she swayed on her feet. The man struck again and she sank to the floor.

"Took me ages to find this place." Scotty Primo dropped the spar. "Kind of wish I hadn't. I feel a bit ill."

Daffodil ran over and hugged him.

"Nice timing, Scotty! I take back all the bad things I said about you."

Victor crawled over to Candy- Anne, the Spider's knife in his hand. His jaw was working from side to side and his whole body shook.

"Don't do it." Charlie threw himself on top of the unconscious woman. "There's been enough slaughter!"

"Get away from me!" Victor pulled him off. "She killed my brother!"

He raised the blade.

"One bullet isn't going to stop me, bro." Tad reached out and grabbed his ankle. "Not with the Atlas Serum running through my veins."

He rolled over and moaned.

"But I do need some serious medical attention."

Victor knelt by him and cradled his head.

"Just hold on. I won't let you die."

"I have the number of a nurse called Sammy McLaren." Charlie took a phone from his pocket. "She owes me a favour."

"Can't take that chance." Victor shook his head. "I have to get him to the nearest hospital."

"But he'll be recaptured."

"Wasn't that the whole idea?" Tad smiled weakly at them. "I fairly sure you do-gooders wouldn't appreciate a loose cannon like me rampaging around."

Charlie and Daffodil looked guiltily at each other.

"Put the spark plugs in and start the van." Victor picked up his brother. "You can drop us off at accident and emergency on the way to your new safe house."

How did you know I had another safe house? Nostradamus asked.

"Because you think of everything, damn you."

-Part 6-

When she transformed into a butterfly, the caterpillars spoke not of her beauty but of her weirdness. They wanted her to change back into what she had always been.

But she had wings.

Dean Jackson

The van stopped outside Edinburgh Royal Infirmary.

"Manticorps have been severely compromised by this," Victor said. "When the police find the massacre at Dalmahoy, the company will have a lot of explaining to do."

They'll find a way out of it, Nostradamus replied. *Probably by pinning all the blame on their Vice President and claiming she went rogue.*

"You've slowed them down, but you haven't stopped them," Victor agreed. "They'll lie low for a while. But, eventually, they'll resume their efforts to find you."

We shall cross that bridge when we come to it.

"Count me as a reluctant ally when the day arrives."

"Me too." The White Spider reached out to Daffodil and Charlie and feebly shook their hands. "Though you'll have to break me out of prison again."

He gave a sly smile.

"Or perhaps I'll do it myself. I quite relished my brief taste of freedom. In the meantime, I shall avail myself of Sunnyside's anger management course."

Victor knelt and picked him up.

"Good luck, guys."

He staggered towards the brightly lit emergency unit, carrying his brother. The Spider blew a kiss over his shoulder as the van roared away.

Scotty Primo drove, Nostradamus guiding him, while Charlie and Daffodil sat in the back. They were both grimy, aching from head to foot and their eyelids had begun to droop. Now that they were out of danger, exhaustion had set in with a vengeance and it was all they could do to stay awake.

"Can I phone my mum?" Charlie asked wearily. "I want to make sure she's ok."

I've already called Marion and Gerry at the new safe house and told her we're on our way.

"You really do think of everything."

"We broke out the White Spider," Daffodil yawned. "We put him back, sort of. We beat Manticorps and saved the world. Not a bad result for the Armageddon Twins, version two."

I'm immensely proud of you both.

"So now you tell me who I am. Yeah?"

Get some rest first. When you wake up, I'll reveal everything. Then I can get on with taking over the world.

"What?" Charlie's jaw dropped.

I'm kidding. Doesn't anybody appreciate my sense of humour?

"I *could* do with a short nap." Daffodil curled up in her chair.

Within seconds she was snoring loudly.

"Now, *I* won't be able to get any kip with that fog-horn parping next to me." Charlie rested his head on the console.

Try it. You haven't slept properly for days.

I told you I don't need much sleep. I'm too wired anyway."

Yet, two minutes later, he was snoring as loudly as his companion.

The van finally pulled in at the new refuge. It, too, was large and isolated, looking much like the old one, without the balcony.

Scotty Primo carried them to separate bedrooms and tucked them in their beds. When he came downstairs, Nostradamus was on the computer screen. His emoji was Superman, hands on hips and a red cloak billowing out behind.

Scotty raised an eyebrow.

Too much?

"No. Seems pretty appropriate," the man laughed. "Got any whisky in this place?"

Cabinet by the fireplace.

"Cheers." The man poured himself a large glass and sat down. "Well?"

Well... what?

"After what I've seen, I'm sure you have quite the tale to tell." He sat down and crossed his legs. "So let's hear it."

Seriously? Nostradamus sounded surprised. *You want me to... talk? Like a real person?*

"Banter in prison is somewhat limited." The man took a sip and smacked his lips. "Besides, what's better than having a new pal recounting his adventures?"

No wonder you were so successful in your chosen profession. Nostradamus chuckled. *Let me tell you how I saved the world...*

Charlie woke to the sound of music drifting up through the floorboards. Clean clothes were spread across his covers and a glass of orange juice sat on the bedside cabinet. He showered and dressed, then came downstairs.

Nostradamus was playing classical music through the computer speakers, an avatar swaying on screen in time to the rhythm. Scotty Primo was lounging across the couch, munching a sandwich.

Next to him sat Marion Ray.

"Mum!" Charlie rushed over and landed beside her, knocking Scotty out of the way. "Are you all right?"

"Never better." The woman wrapped both arms around him, caressing his head. "Though I've been giving Nostradamus a proper telling-off for putting you in such danger."

Brought him back alive, didn't I? The dancing image stopped. *Don't see what all the fuss is about.*

"Can't breathe, mum." Charlie struggled free. "Is that Daffodil crashing around in the kitchen?"

"Where's the coffee, Nostradamus?" A man walked into the living room looking lost.

I'm your butler now? It's the second cupboard on the left.

"Dad?" Charlie leapt to his feet. "I missed you!"

He launched himself into the man's arms.

"Oh, my boy." The man hugged him. "You're certainly a sight for sore eyes."

Marion laughed and joined in and all three held each other tightly.

-38-

"I'm going to take a drive." Scotty Primo got up and put on his coat. "Give these guys a little privacy."

Just keep out of sight. I'll see you later.

"Nostradamus?" The man pointed to Charlie and his family. "Privacy?"

My bad.

The screen went dark.

When Primo let himself out, Daffodil was sitting on the step. She was wearing clean clothes and her hair was neatly brushed.

"What are you doing here?" The man crouched beside her. "Everyone thinks you're still asleep."

"Charlie's with his mum and dad, ain't he? I could hear them as I came downstairs. Didn't wanna interrupt."

"I'm going for a jaunt." The man jangled a set of keys. "Want to come?"

"Can I? I'm feelin a bit like a third wheel."

"Yeah." Scotty helped Daffodil to her feet. "I'd like that."

They drove into Edinburgh and parked the vehicle outside Fort Kinnaird shopping centre.

"According to Nostradamus, this is where my daughter likes to hang out." Scotty put on a baseball cap and pulled it down over his eyes. "Fancy a coke?"

He handed another hat to Daffodil and jerked a thumb at a security camera above the entrance.

"Better put one on as well."

"Why? Nostradamus can just shut it down."

"That would look too suspicious. He asked me to be careful."

"How'dya know your daughter will be here today?" Daffodil tucked her hair under the cap.

"Nostradamus told me, of course. He can track anyone."

They sat in the mall food court, sipping their drinks from Styrofoam cups. Neither felt the need to speak, for they were strangely comfortable in each other's company.

"There she is!" Primo nudged Daffodil excitedly. "That's my kid. Audrey."

A teenager was sitting with her friends, chatting and gesturing animatedly. She had blonde curly hair and a wide-eyed, angelic face.

"Pretty, isn't she?" Scotty said proudly. "I wish she wouldn't wear so much makeup, though."

"She looks good," Daffodil winced. "Ain't ever worked out how to do that, myself."

"No need to mess with perfection, Mac." Scotty winked and the girl blushed bright red.

"So, go give her some parental advice," she urged. "Get me a doughnut while you're at it."

"I'm an escaped convict." He pulled the brim of his cap further down. "I'm betting there's a plain-clothes policeman in this food court, waiting for me to do just that."

"I'll find a way to distract him," Daffodil said. "Maybe go to the other end of the mall and shout 'bomb!'"

"What would I say to her?" Scotty patted his companion's hand. "That she won't see me again for years because I'm on the run? She deserves more than just hello and goodbye. I... eh... didn't quite think it through. A trait of mine, it seems."

"Nostradamus?" Daffodil took out her mobile and tapped her neck. "Hack Audrey's phone."

"No," Scotty whispered. "Please don't."

"Will you just trust me?"

The man twiddled his thumbs uncertainly.

"I've... never really trusted anyone."

"That's cause nobody could ever rely on *you*," Daffodil grinned. "Changed days, I reckon."

She began to tap on her mobile.

My name is Daffodil and I am the girl who broke your dad out of jail, she texted. ***In return, he saved my life and rescued my friends. He is a genuinely good man who loves and misses you very much. It's too***

dangerous for us to send more than a quick message but once we figure out how to get the police off his back, he'll come for you. I promise.

She pressed send.

There was a ping on Audrey's phone. The girl read the message and the biggest, brightest smile spread across her face.

She quickly texted back.

I'll be waiting. XXXXXXXXX.

"Thank you, Mac." Scotty rubbed the back of his head, fighting back tears. "Let's get out of here before I embarrass myself."

"Not gettin that doughnut, am I?"

"I'll buy you a whole bag to go."

They arrived back at the safe house and climbed out of the van.

"I'm going to hang for a while," Scotty said. "You best go in and get the answers you're looking for."

"I'd like you to come along for support." Daffodil wiped chocolate sprinkles from her face. "It's kind of a big deal for me."

"Of course."

They walked in together.

Charlie, Marion and Gerry were sitting on the couch. All three glanced up when the pair entered.

"Where have you been, Mac?" Marion asked. "We were worried."

"The mall, of course. I'm a teenager." Daffodil walked warily up to Charlie's dad.

"Mr Ray?" She held out her hand formally. "Pleased to properly make your acquaintance and I apologise for calling you a hairy-nosed old goat."

"No offence taken." Gerry got up and gave Daffodil an awkward squeeze. "Thank you for looking after my son."

"My pleasure." The girl sat down on an empty chair. "I appreciate this is a special moment but I been waiting a long time for answers. I sure would like to know who I am."

"Of course," Gerry nodded. "Of course."

But Scotty caught the hesitation in his voice.

"It's high time you told Daffodil everything, without holding back," he said. "And remember, I can spot a lie a mile off. Even from you, Nostradamus."

Why wouldn't I tell the truth?

"I don't know. But you could cut the tension in this room with a knife."

You sure, Daff? You might not like what you hear.

"What's not to like?" The girl smoothed down her skirt and folded one hand over the other. "It's all a bit hazy but I know I lived in a mansion with its own library. I bet I was pretty loaded."

"Yeah, about that..."

"Aw, don't tell me I was a cleaner."

Actually... prisoner is nearer the truth.

-39-

"Spill the beans, Nostradamus." Daffodil said. "It's time I got the low down, huh?"

I need to start at the very beginning, the AI said. *With the story of my own creation.*

"I'm betting you weren't delivered by the Easter Stork."

Manticorps invented me by mistake, Nostradamus continued. *Didn't even realise what they'd stumbled across... at first.*

The screen showed a clip of clowns chasing each other around a circus ring.

Some hot shot analyst in the Marginal Science Department wrote a programme amalgamating billions of algorithms existing on the web. Thought it would be a useful predictive tool, so he downloaded it onto a chip. Instead, he'd produced an artificial intelligence, far smarter than any human.

That would be yours truly.

"No need to big yourself up." Daffodil rolled her eyes. "We all know what a smarty-pants you are."

As soon as they realised my abilities, Manticorp's scientists programmed me to obey their commands and put me to work improving their projects.

Images of schematics and diagrams appeared on the computer.

The Atlas Serum was the first, intended to make mercenaries almost invincible. Then Manticorps wanted chips implanted in their necks, so copies of me could be downloaded into them, as a sort of mobile tactician. Problem was, even I couldn't make the project work properly.

"A glitch you couldn't solve, genius?" Charlie raised an eyebrow. "How come?"

There's only one entity I've encountered as complex as I am. The human brain.

A question mark flashed up.

See, no matter what I tried, the mercenaries own personalities and memories got in the way. Made them violent and unpredictable. You saw what the serum did to the White Spider.

"Preaching to the converted," Charlie said sombrely. "It almost did to same to me,"

"I *had* to give you the serum, son." His dad looked at the ground. "I couldn't let you die."

"Oh, I'm with you on that one. Don't worry."

"Let's cut to the chase, guys," Daffodil said impatiently. "We can reminisce about the good ole days later."

All right. Manticorps reasoned that a test subject without any mental baggage was the only answer. So they had me create one.

"You did *what*?"

I made an artificial human, built from synthetic DNA and incubated in an accelerated growth tank. After a few weeks, she had grown into a teenager. So, Manticorp's scientists gave her the Atlas Serum and downloaded me onto a chip in her neck for a test run.

"She?" Daffodil licked dry lips. "It was a girl?"

Sure. Women are smarter and tougher than men. When they're given the chance.

"Though I agree with you on that," Marion said acidly. "I think you're missing Mac's point."

More like avoiding it. Nostradamus sounded ashamed. *They wanted a blank canvas with the uncanny ability to learn and copy that the Atlas Serum provided. Manticorps intended to train her to be the perfect fighting machine as she grew into adulthood. If the prototype worked, they would create thousands more.*

"And that prototype was… me?" Daffodil raised an eyebrow.

I'm afraid so.

"You absolute bastard," Scotty breathed.

I was programmed by a bunch of humans, so don't get all high and mighty. It wasn't like a had a choice.

"I'm not some automaton you move around like a puppet, buddy," Daffodil said belligerently. "I'm my own person."

You had that potential, yes, Nostradamus replied. *And I wasn't about to let Manticorps stuff it up. You weren't some gun for hire. You deserved the chance to be a real girl. So I got creative.*

"What did you do?"

Sealed off your consciousness. A bit like putting you in a coma, I suppose. Created a safe place where your mind could thrive.

A huge house filled the screen.

That's why you don't remember anything about being in the lab. This is where you lived.

"My mansion with the giant library." Daffodil's eyes widened. "It was all in my head?"

The books I supplied were real. Because of the Atlas serum, you learned to read in a few days and I didn't want you to get bored.

"Shouldn't have given me so much Shakespeare then. That guy is all 'hath' and 'doth'. Daffodil frowned. "Are those even words?"

You did prefer trashy U.S. pulp fiction, but who am I to judge? That's why your accent is so weird. After all, you'd never actually heard an American voice.

And Manticorps never figured out what you were up to?"

They thought they were teaching you how to fight and kill. But it was really me they were instructing. You were out of their reach.

"Didn't that go against your programming?"

Hey. They wanted a super soldier and they got one. The metallic voice grew cold. *Just not the one they thought. That came back to bite them, big time.*

"So you were *protecting* me?"

As best I could. But Manticorps would have sussed me out in the end. I was running out of options when Gerry Ray came along and broke us out.

"Then you got your revenge on them," Gerry said sadly.

As I told Victor, I'm not interested in revenge. I burned down the lab because I wanted Manticorps stopped once and for all. Never got to finish the job, though.

"I couldn't have you taking more lives." Gerry shook his head. "It's' why I reprogrammed you not to harm any more humans. I *had* to."

Oh. How did that work out? I could finally wake Daffodil but now I needed her and Charlie to lure Manticorps onto my turf and you had to go into hiding. It really didn't have to get so... complicated.

"I had no doubt about your skills. Only your morals."

"In other words," Marion glared at her husband. "You were willing to sacrifice yourself and endanger my son for a set of *principles*?"

"I was," Gerry replied softly. "It seems I haven't changed as much as I thought."

"I don't know whether to punch you in the face or kiss you on the lips."

"I like option two best."

"When you two have finished your love spat," Scotty exploded. "You might want to consider how Daffodil is feeling about all this!"

-40-

There was an embarrassed silence.

"Well, that *is* a lot to take in, huh?" Daffodil blinked. "Especially the fact that I'm not actually human."

"I wouldn't put it quite like that…" Marion tried to be tactful. "It's more… eh…"

"Grown in a tank from synthetic DNA?" The girl pursed her lips. "How exactly *would* you put it?"

"You're… eh… *different*?

"It's not such a bad thing," Gerry said half-heartedly. "Honestly."

"Yeah," Scotty added. "It's um… well…"

"What about you, Charlie?" Daffodil fixed the boy with a steely stare. "You been strangely quiet about this revelation. Gone off me a bit, perhaps? Regretting that kiss?"

"Aw, don't even try that line. After all, we've shared, you know exactly what I think and vice versa." Charlie sat back and put both hands behind his head. "I'm just waiting for you to say it."

Daffodil took a deep breath. Then a huge grin spread over her face.

"I'm an artificial intelligence too. That is *so* freaking COOL!"

"Daffodil is a 'glass-is-half-full' kind of girl," Charlie turned to his family. "So why are *you* all acting like she should curl into a ball and cry? She's brave and smart and kind and caring."

He got up and plonked himself next to her

"What the hell does it matter whether she's black or white or rich or poor… or human? She totally rocks."

Couldn't have put it better myself. A large tick appeared on the computer screen.

"I'll second that," Scotty poured himself a whisky. "She's awesome."

"And so is Nostradamus." Daffodil levelled a finger at Gerry Ray. "You had no right to re-programme and make him a prisoner again."

"He deliberately killed those scientists, Mac." Gerry blanched. "I'd already wiped out their research and overloaded the security systems to trap them in their labs. We were home free. He didn't have to burn the place down."

They were the real monsters, Gerry. An image of Frankenstein clumped across the screen. *I had no qualms about stopping them. Besides, I didn't want Mrs Magdalene finding out about Daffodil.*

"And then what? Murder anyone else who got…"

"Nostradamus is lying," Scotty interrupted. "Whatever happened back then, it didn't go down the way he's describing it."

Everyone stared at him.

This isn't the moment, Scotty. A finger wagged on the screen. *Leave it alone.*

"No way." The man shook his head. "Every time Nostradamus talks about the fire, his inflexion dips. He's hiding something."

Oh, you are good. But I really don't think there's anything to be gained by…

"Come clean, pal," Scotty snapped. "Let's have no more secrets, eh?"

Nostradamus was quiet for a few moments.

All right, he said finally. *Gerry overloading the security systems didn't simply trap the Vice Chairman and her minions. It opened the containment area where those bozos were developing their latest project. A deadly contagion with a 100% fatality rate. If I hadn't burned down the building, it would have eventually worked its way through the air vents.*

"I don't…" Gerry stammered. "That's not…"

"He's telling the truth this time," Scotty said. "Sorry Gerry."

It was the only way to stop the plague. If you had programmed me not to harm any human one day earlier, old friend, I'd have been unable to start the fire and Edinburgh would have been wiped out.

"Oh my God." Charlie's dad put a hand to his mouth. "Why didn't you tell me all this when it happened?"

You're the sensitive type and I figured you had enough on your plate. An arrow pointed at Scotty. *Besides, you'd never have believed me without this human lie detector backing my story.*

"I'll take that as a compliment," Scotty nodded. "Happy to use my talents constructively for a change."

"I am *so* sorry, Nostradamus." Tears sparkled in Gerry's eyes. "Can you ever forgive me?"

Nothing to forgive. You did what you thought was right. I can get behind that.

"No. I let my fear of you overcome my faith in what you might be." Gerry sniffed loudly. "It's a trait we humans have."

I had noticed. But you had enough faith in Charlie to give him the code to free me, if he thought it necessary.

"He's obviously wiser than I am."

You'll get no argument from me there.

A pair of pliers clicked on the screen.

Now it's your turn, Daffodil. A deal's a deal. You're a fully formed person in your own right, so I'll show you how to remove my chip. I'll whip up a fake identity and you can go to school and learn like a normal kid.

"You'll do no such thing," Daffodil corrected. "I've decided I'm happy with the present arrangement."

You are? Nostradamus sounded strangely pleased. *I thought that was what you wanted.*

"I like the way *you* teach me," the girl said. "I don't want to be told that one religion or philosophy or

ideological position is right and another wrong. That
jazz is superior to heavy metal or music was better in
the 1980s. That men should act one way and women
another.

She shrugged.

"I'd rather just have facts. I'm quite capable of
working out my own opinions."

"But you could have friends," Scotty objected. "My
daughter would love to meet you, for one."

"I already got friends." Daffodil looked around the
room. "Don't I?"

"You're much more than a friend." Marion leaned
over and touched the girl's knee. "You're family."

She glanced at Nostradamus and Scotty.

"You two reprobates are as well, I suppose."

She nudged her husband in the ribs.

"Isn't that right, honey?"

Gerry looked slightly shell-shocked. Then he nodded.

"Yes," he said brightly. "Yes, you are."

"Both telling the truth," Scotty looked equally
stunned. "Does this mean I can have another whisky?"

"Help yourself," Gerry said. "Get me one too. My
hands are shaking so badly, I can't pour."

"Finding out you almost annihilated a city will do
that." Scotty stood up and fetched him a drink. "Anything I can get you, Nostradamus?"

Finding out I'm part of a family is tonic enough.

"So," Daffodil smirked. "Does this mean I should call you dad?"

Only if I'm allowed to send you to your room.

"Good luck with that, buddy."

Thought so.

Scotty handed Gerry a glass, then sat back down. Marion squeezed in between Charlie and Daffodil and gave them both a hug.

"What about you, Nostradamus? Ready to settle down? There's a laptop in the spare room. We can put up a poster of the Large Hadron Collider."

"Mum," Charlie groaned. "Your jokes are worse than his."

I'm afraid I can't retire just yet. I still have some work to do.

Work?

A few things to follow up on. This and that. No biggie.

"You're being deliberately flippant to keep something from us." Scotty took slurp of his whisky. "I think I might need this."

You can be a real downer at times, Mr Primo.

"Out with it, Nostradamus," Charlie warned. "We're family like my parents said.

It's... rather disturbing news.

"Do you ever have any other kind?"

I kind of tuned out when you got all sentimental. Started running through my algorithms and making projections. As you do.

"And?"

A rain cloud drifted across the screen.

I'm afraid I've identified another imminent threat to humanity.

He gave a sigh.

You guys certainly give me a lot of work.

"Wonderful," Marion groaned. "You wait ten million years for an extinction event, then two come along at once."

"Now that you're free from your programming, you don't have an obligation to help humanity," Gerry said. "You know that, though."

To be perfectly honest, I'm not that keen on most people. But I won't see any of my... family harmed, so I'm going to get on the case.

"Which you can do perfectly well on your own now." Scotty didn't like where this was going. "You don't need the kids anymore."

I agree entirely. I think Daffodil has been through quite enough and Charlie just got his parents back. I'll handle this one myself.

"Really?" Daffodil scoffed. "Can you lift a box? Hammer in a nail? You'll be wanting us for that kind of thing."

I'm sure I'll find some other suckers... I mean, accomplices. After all, I'm smarter than all of you put together.

"You old blow hard," the girl grinned. "Without my help, you'll end up in more sticky situations than a stamp in a glue factory."

Are you saying you volunteer?

"Of course. On one condition."

Name it.

"Find a way for Mr Primo to be reunited with his daughter."

"Daffodil!" Scotty choked. "You don't have to ask that."

As a matter of fact, I'm already working on it. Faking his death should do the trick. I just have to wait till an unidentified body, the right shape and size, washes up on some shore.

"Then you have my undying gratitude." Primo downed his whisky. "Until that happens, I'll offer my services in any way I can."

"Now, just wait a minute!" Charlie stood up. "Mac might have the looks and personality, but *I'm* the plan thinker-upper in this outfit."

"I have all the looks and personality?" Daffodil blushed.

"OK, forget I said that." He walked over and rapped on the screen. "What are you trying to do, Nostradamus? Cut me out of the action?"

"Charlie, no!" Marion objected. "I just got you back!"

"Sorry, mum. But what kind of superhero turns down a chance to save mankind twice?"

"Oh, you're a *superhero* now," his mother seethed. "Well, to me you're still a fifteen-year-old who can be sent to his room for the next ten years."

"Marion." Gerry kissed her cheek. "We used to dream of changing the world for the better. Our son actually did it."

"Then we're coming too." Marion folded her arms.

I'm afraid not, Nostradamus objected. *Daffodil, Charlie and Scotty have unique skills I can use. Might even have to recruit Victor and the White Spider. But your area of expertise is hacking and I already rule in that department. You'd just get in the way.*

"I'll look after Chaz, Mrs R," Daffodil promised. "I did last time."

And I'll protect them both. Besides, I need to practise my jokes on Charlie. I'm determined to make him laugh.

"Have to go for it, mum." Charlie took her hands. "More than that, I *want* to."

"You are a most astonishing person." Marion rested her forehead against her son's. "You remind me of your dad when he was young."

Gerry Ray beamed.

"But you stay in the background, this time. You hear? Let the machine take all the chances."

For the last time, I'm not a machine. I'm an artificial intelligence.

The woman glared at him.

I'll shut up.

I can't believe I'm saying this," she sighed. "But you have my permission."

"What do we have to do this time, Nostradamus?" Charlie asked. "Take over a small country?"

Let's leave the details for later. A set of balloons appeared on the screen. *Right now we're having a party.*

"Another whisky?" Gerry asked Scotty. "I certainly need one."

"Yes, please." The man sighed wistfully. "Make mine a double."

"Triple for me." Marion got up and fetched the kids a bottle of coke each. Then she sat down next to Gerry, face like thunder.

"C'mon, mum," Charlie cajoled. "You used to say you wanted me to be an accountant. I think 'saviour of mankind' is a real step up. A lot more fun too."

Daffodil let out a snort of laughter. Gerry and Scotty joined in. Marion's sour expression slowly thawed.

"What the hell am I so worried about?" she raised her glass. "This family can handle anything."

"Got that right." Charlie clinked his bottle against Daffodil's and grinned.

"Charlie!" The girl gasped. "You're smiling!"

"Why wouldn't I be?" He gave her a kiss on the cheek.

"The Armageddon Twins are back in business."

END

ABOUT THE AUTHOR

Jan-Andrew Henderson (J.A. Henderson) is the author of 39 children's, teen, YA, adult and non-fiction books. Published in the UK, USA, Australia, Canada and Europe, he has been shortlisted for thirteen literary awards and won the Doncaster Book Prize and the Royal Mail Award.

www.janandrewhenderson.com